I0537697

ALTER BOYS

Tory Allyn

NOVELS
ALTER EGO
ALTER BOYS*

*Book two in my series: THE DAVENPORT DECREES

Table of Contents

Chapter 1

Deep, rich hues ascended along the mountainous peaks as tawdry affairs and paid by the hour fares gathered their evening wares. Nobody relishes the walk of shame so out of their rooms they came as the darkness cloaked an anonymous name. Even though doors slammed and engines revved, nothing disturbed the detectives dead asleep in their beds. Soon another morning will wipe away the grime and cease all crime at the notorious Interstate Inn.

It had been a long, strenuous day for them. After executing legwork for FBI Special Agent Jack Stanwick, and their boss, Raymond Davenport, they had listened in on a disturbing conversation between four men at Prescott Chemicals. If that weren't enough, all three fell into a vat of liquid that needed to be showered off so a sordid motel room became their home for the evening. The guys were mighty tired.

Russ tossed and turned to find a comfortable position but instead felt the pangs of distress that were experienced earlier in the night. It was soon followed by moaning and groaning so he grabbed hold of his stomach, hurried out of bed and dashed into the bathroom. The door was locked behind him.

As the pain subsided, a tingling sensation began from his head straight to the toes. Again, the grandfather's emerald ring pinged against the tile, alerting him to what has transpired. With a quick feel over the entire body, a prolonged scream permeated the motel room. Russ dropped to the floor in hysterics. Bren and Derek woke up, scrambled out of bed and banged on the bathroom door.

"What's going on in there?"

"Russ, are you ok? Derek grasped the locked door knob.

"Like, no!" The sobbing sounded excruciating.

Bren looked at Derek. "Was that a woman's voice I just heard."

They pounded on the door.

"Open up, Russ," Derek yowled. "I told you not to lock this bathroom door.

"Do you have a woman in there?" Bren yelled.

"Unlock this door!" Derek roared.

Bren sneered. "You better not be using our towels!"

"Like, I've wrapped my own around me," squawked a feminine voice. "I so don't want you to see me this way."

"There is a woman in there," Bren snarled.

"Open this door now!" Derek ordered. "Or I'm calling Raymond."

"No, please don't," came her crying plea. "I'm totally unlocking it now."

Once the click was heard, Derek flung it open.

"It's pitch-dark in here," Bren bellowed.

"Let me get it!" Derek switched on the light.

They jumped back with their mouths wide open as both simultaneously whipped the palms against their boxer shorts, covering up the private parts.

"Who the hell are you?" Derek belted out.

Sobbing hysterically, the woman squealed in a high-pitched tone, "Like, I'm Russ!"

"Nonsense..." Bren yanked open the shower curtain. "He's not in there."

Derek clenched his jaw as he looked at the trembling woman. "I'm in no mood for games. Where's Russ?"

"Like, I am Russ," she implored. "You've so got to believe me."

Bren looked at Derek. "He...she...whomever this person is, they're playing a trick on us."

"I'm so not playing tricks," she screamed. "It's me, totally...for real!"

2

Derek stuck his head out and looked in Russ' bed. "He's not in his bed."

"You need to stop this!" Bren slammed his foot on the floor. "This is not funny."

Derek leaned and looked into her eyes. "Miss, don't play games, please. You're kind of scaring me."

With tears gushing from her eyes, she said with a fractured voice, "Like, I'm so sorry!"

Russ is pulling a fast one," Bren groused. He walked out of the bathroom. "He brought one of his chicks, as he calls them, into our room to play a dirty trick on us. I know it. I bet you he's outside this motel door."

Derek looked on.

Bren grabbed the handle and opened it. The night was cold and quiet as he put his head out. After searching both ways, he darted to the car, gave it the once over then hurried back inside.

"I knew he wouldn't be out there," Derek remarked.

"The moron is probably under one of the beds." Bren headed toward them.

Derek pulled open the closet. "He's not in here."

"Nor under the beds." Bren shook his head.

"Where else could Russ be?" Derek shrugged.

"I don't know," Bren reacted. "But mark my words, he's up to something."

"In the meantime..." Derek pointed in the bathroom. "There's a naked woman crying her eyes out."

"Russ is good at goading us," Bren stated.

Derek walked into the bathroom with his hand out. "He's not that good."

The girl sat on the floor bitterly weeping. "Like, I'm Russ. Please, you've got to totally believe me!"

"He has pulled so many pranks on us." Bren snapped his fingers. "I know..." He leaned close to Derek's ear. "We can ask her some personal questions about ourselves."

3

"Yeah..." He turned toward Russ, who was sobbing. "Miss, Miss—"

She looked up.

"Can I ask you something?"

The girl had tears streaming down her face as she replied, "Like, totally."

"What's my favorite color?" Derek asked.

She sniveled then took a deep breath. "Green."

He looked at Bren. "It's right."

"Ask another?"

Derek turned back. "What's my middle name?"

"Patrick," she replied.

Bren pushed him aside. "Ok, Miss smarty-pants, what are mine?"

Whimpering, she replied, "Your favorite color is burgundy and your middle name is Alexander."

"I'll give you that, but what is my sister's name?" Bren prodded.

She sniffled. "Tabby, which is short for Tabitha."

Panic removed Bren's smug expression. His head rapidly turned to face Derek, who appeared bewildered. He swung it back around and looked at the woman. Her lips were quivering.

"What's happening?" he shouted out.

Derek flew by Bren and grabbed Russ. He slung his arms around her. "I'm sorry, Russ. I'm really sorry."

Her arms shook as she put them around him. "Like, I totally am too."

As the hysterical minutes flew by, they slowly calmed themselves down. Russ left the embrace of Derek, walked out to a chair by the window and recovered the T-shirt which was now dry. She removed the towel and tossed the garment over her shoulders. It dropped to nightgown length at mid-thigh.

"Like, oh my God," she cried out. "I'm way smaller, and my fierce muscles are gone."

4

Derek rushed over and gave her a huge hug. "You wouldn't want all that bulk to ruin your hot body."

She pulled the T-shirt tightly against her figure. "I do have a blazing bod, don't I?"

"Russ..." She turned her head.

Bren snapped a few pictures on his digital camera.

"Really?" Derek yelled.

"It's called evidence." Bren placed the camera into his satchel. "After all, I am a detective."

"Then use your skills to figure out what we should do..." Derek huffed. "Since you're supposedly the brains of our outfit."

"I am." He paced the floor. "Let me think a second."

Derek spoke up. "What about the hospital?"

"Thank you," Bren reacted. "I never would have thought of that."

Derek smirked. "That's sarcasm, isn't it?"

"You think?" Bren flung out his hand. "I know, we'll tell the attending physician that our friend just suddenly and unexplainably turned from a man into a woman in the bathroom of a seedy motel, and we were wondering if you had a pill, shot or suppository that would change our friend back into the fun-loving dude he once was!"

"Now, that is definitely sarcasm," Derek remarked.

"Wait a minute..." Bren hopped on the bed and grabbed a cell phone out of his satchel. "Thank the sweet Lord this wasn't with me when we were drenched. I'll give Raymond a call." He dialed. "He'll know exactly what to do."

"Awesome!" Derek laid Russ on the bed and covered her up. "You need to rest."

"I totally can't," she uttered.

Derek climbed in next to her. "Just try."

She closed her eyes.

"Hello, Raymond? It's Bren, and we have a huge problem. I'm putting you on speaker phone."

"What's going on?"

5

"I'm really not sure—"

"What?"

Bren exhaled. "I have no idea how to tell you this."

"Just tell me."

He cleared his throat. "Russ has turned into a woman."

"What did you just say?"

"Russ has turned into a woman," Bren enunciated.

"I thought that's what I heard," Raymond stated. "I cannot believe it."

"I am telling you the truth."

"I'd never doubt you," Raymond maintained. "Now Russ on the other hand—"

"You'd take him with a grain of salt."

"Ask him what we should do?" Derek requested.

"We thought about bringing him to the hospital but that would never work," Bren noted.

"No, don't do that," Raymond insisted. "I'll have to call my friend, Dr. Munson, and tell him about your predicament," he said. "I'll call right back. Just hold tight."

As the dial tone blared, Bren hung up.

Derek looked over at Russ, who appeared to be sleeping.

"Raymond will take care of this," Bren claimed. "I just know it."

"We don't know what we're dealing with here," Derek countered. "I doubt that Dr. Munson will either."

"We just have to hope and pray he does," Bren lamented.

Derek nodded. "Yeah, for our sake."

A few tense minutes had gone by when finally the cell phone rang. Bren hit the speaker button. "Hello?"

"Boys, I'm en route to pick up Dr. Munson." It was Raymond. "Where are you?"

"We are at the Interstate Inn, room twelve," Bren replied. "The motel is just off I-95 on Rt. 80 in Cantor County."

6

"Call me if things become worse," Raymond issued. "We'll be there shortly."

Bren hung up and looked at Derek. "Good, they will be here soon."

"Soon?" Derek uttered. "Soon at best is an hour away and Raymond drives like an old lady."

"The way he sounded, there will be no old woman on the road tonight." Bren tried to sound convincing.

Russ woke and began to uncontrollably shake. She threw the covers off as the guys watched her enlarge. Her hair shortened as the face lost its womanly softness. Even the fuzzy facial hair and sideburns came in. The shoulders became masculine again as her breasts returned to a chest. The arms began to grow and churn out blonde hair. The legs came back to their muscular size and his male genitalia returned to its normal girth. The T-shirt fit like a glove.

"Oh, man." Derek got off the bed.

Bren stood in place with his jaw askew.

Russ jumped up. "Dudes, I'm majorly back!" His virile voice vocalized.

Derek gave him a hearty bear-hug. "Awesome."

"Like, totally—"

"Hopefully, a little nicer," Bren quipped. "And for heaven's sake, put some underwear on."

Derek let go. "Man, I didn't even notice."

Russ laughed, put on his boxers and headed toward the bathroom to look at the results. As he stared at every inch and examined all his body parts, a grin came over his face. It looked like nothing ever took place. He exited and went up to Bren and Derek.

"Like, I can't believe that just happened to me."

"Me either," Derek added.

"Remember the men at Prescott Chemicals talking about a formula they were to use on somebody and how it would make his masculine feelings become feminine—"

"Totally."

7

"What if the vat we fell into contained that formula?" Bren surmised.

Russ looked at Derek.

"It would make perfect sense."

Derek nodded. "The whole kit and caboodle was all lit up with dials moving every which way—"

"And that grody liquid was all warm and stank-smelling." Russ recalled.

"We could have absorbed some into our systems," Bren thought aloud.

"Like, I got some way in my mouth." Russ squirmed.

Derek's face puckered. "Me too."

"I also did," Bren added.

"So this could happen to us too?" Derek clamored.

"It could—"

"It will..." Derek shot back. "And when it does, I'm going to freak out."

Bren huffed. "You need to calm down."

"Yeah, sure," Derek uttered. "The thing is we could change at any time. Who knows? If not today, maybe it'll be tomorrow, next week, a month or even a year."

"Just stop dwelling on it," Bren insisted.

"But we could be at the post office, eating at a restaurant or even shopping in a grocery store grabbing a box of cereal then bam!" Derek snapped "You're a woman."

"Like, clean up in aisle seven," Russ blurted out.

Bren gave him a dirty look then turned back to Derek. "You need to stop agonizing over it. You'll put yourself into an early grave thinking about it, or even worse—"

"What's worse?"

"Worrying so much that you go prematurely gray," he replied. "You don't want that if you're a woman."

8

"Oh, aren't you funny," Derek quipped. "Funny-looking, that is." He smirked. "Why are you so calm?"

"This turning into a woman thing might never happen to me, and if it does, I'll deal with it then," Bren retorted. "Since Russ went through it and appears to be well—albeit still an idiot—I think I'll handle it just fine."

"You don't know what this is doing to our bodies..." Derek fumed. "We could get very sick, die or lose our manhood and stay a woman."

"I so don't want to lose my manhood," Russ uttered. "Like, its way needed for recreational purposes. My babes would majorly suffer."

"If you become a woman, just some of your babes would suffer," Bren countered. "Besides, you like them kinky."

Russ smirked. "Dude, it's called freaky."

"Is that the politically-correct term for it these days?" Bren asked. "At this point, I don't care. I'm going back to bed."

"C'mon, Russ. I'll get in bed with you and we can watch a movie." Derek offered. "It'll be awhile before Raymond and Dr. Munson get here."

"Cool, dude." Russ dropped his boxers and crawled underneath the covers. "You're so rad."

Derek climbed into bed. "I'm awesomely rad!"

Both faced each other and sniggered.

"I think Bren is taking this too lightly," Derek said. "He can go to that hard place, but I cannot."

"I totally can't either."

"We don't know what this is doing to our insides," Derek repeated. "I saw what it can do to our outsides. Seeing you as a woman freaked me the hell out. That could happen to me. The question is when?"

"How am I going to get any sleep with you two buffoons babbling on?" Bren sat up. "I thought a quiet movie was going to be watched. Emphasis on the quiet."

"We will, as soon as we're done talking," Derek replied.

"Like, chitchat soothes me, so shut your hole," Russ demanded.

Bren snickered. "Oh, you do need to relax."

9

"I was completely chill until your backtalk," Russ declared.

"Bren, go back to sleep," Derek urged.

"Let's pretend I got some in the first place," he stated. "Besides, I'm not tired."

"Well, we're going to talk," Derek remarked.

"What about?" Bren asked. "Your lives?"

"Maybe," Derek responded. "They could take a very sharp turn into something we know nothing about.

"Oh, you'll adapt!" Bren snarled. "We all would have to. There's no other choice."

Derek looked at Russ. "What did it feel like to be a woman?"

"It totally felt like me, just way prettier."

Bren sneered. "He's definitely back!"

"How did you see yourself if you were on the floor in the dark?" Derek questioned.

Russ swallowed. "Like, remember when I was on the floor the first time covered with the wet towels?"

Both promptly nodded.

"I had wicked cramps, so I totally grabbed my tummy and hurried into the bathroom—"

"Was it the runs?" Derek interjected.

"Yes, from his mouth!" Bren chuckled.

Derek glared at him. "Seriously?"

Bren scowled. "Don't be such a killjoy."

"Your joy isn't the only thing I'm going to kill," Derek remarked. He faced Russ. "Go ahead and tell us the rest."

"Like, I sat on the closed toilet seat and was totally doubled-over then my face felt way weird. So I got up and looked into the mirror and watched myself way change into a woman. That's when my grandpa's ring fell off..." He jumped out of bed and rushed to the bathroom.

"Is it happening again?" Derek yelled out.

Russ came out with the ring securely back on his finger. "Nope, just had to find where this baby was majorly sitting." He displayed it to them.

"Would you wear some boxer shorts to bed?" Bren grimaced. "Nobody wants to see all that yuck flopping to and fro."

Russ turned around. "Like, how about all this?" He shook his bubble-butt for all to see.

"Blah..." Bren's tongue flew out. "Double yuck!"

Russ leaped back into bed.

Derek laughed. "You two remind me of my brothers."

Bren leaned forward. "How do you mean?"

"I have an older brother, Brayden, who is very smart. My younger brother, Royce, is the sassy one. As the middle child, I had to constantly break up arguments between them. Some became heated, but others were just mild banter. It's the same with you two. One is the brain and the other the brawn."

Bren snickered. "All of us know which brothers we emulate."

"Yes, but I do not want that role again," Derek maintained.

"Like, he's so telling us to lighten up."

Bren sneered. "You first, chunky."

"After you, bones." Russ jabbed.

"You two make me feel right at home," Derek stated.

"I'm the smart one, so that means you're the sloppy one." Bren pointed to Russ.

"I said sassy, not sloppy." Derek glared at Bren. "Supposedly, for being the smart one, you don't listen very well."

Russ stuck out his tongue.

Bren smirked. "I almost liked you better as a woman. At least it gave me something good to look at," he said. "Now I have to deal with you and your antics."

Russ grabbed his man area. "Dude, deal with this."

"If I do, you'll be back to speaking with your high-pitched shrill," Bren snapped.

11

Russ beamed. "That just totally gave me a cool thought."

"No more callers, folks," Bren announced. "We've got ourselves a winner!"

"Just ignore him and tell me," Derek uttered.

"Like, if we majorly turn into chicks, I've so got our girl names—"

"I already have one picked out for you!" Bren interrupted. "I just wouldn't be able to say it in the company of ladies."

Russ continued unfazed. "Bren, you'll totally become Brie. Derek, your name will be Darla and I'll be Rue."

"You have got to be kidding me—"

"We'll definitely need names if we become girls," Derek chimed in.

Bren scoffed. "That will never happen to me."

"Like, I so bet it will," Russ quipped. "And unlike me, it won't be pretty either."

"It doesn't matter," Bren remarked. "I wouldn't go out in public if that happened—"

"And the world takes a collective sigh of relief!" Derek heckled.

"I'm going back to sleep." Bren turned over. "I suggest you both do the same."

Russ fluffed his pillow. "Like, I could totally go for some shut-eye."

"Brother, you just said a mouthful." Derek shut off the lamp.

Peace and quiet fell over the room.

"At long last, no more blathering yaps!" Bren signed off.

Chapter 2

With Dr. Mitchell Munson in the passenger seat, Raymond Davenport entered the parking lot of the Interstate Inn. Darkness still held a firm grip on the sky. Even the moon rested behind a haze of clouds which dimmed an already gloomy situation.

"Are you sure you have the correct location?" Mitchell asked. "This place appears quite seamy."

Raymond picked up a small piece of paper. "This seems to be the motel."

"We should continue on," Dr. Munson urged.

While the headlights turned from low to high beams, the car crept further back until Bren's vehicle came into view. They pulled up next to it, got out and went up to the door.

"Here's their room," Raymond stated.

"Twelve," Dr. Munson said. "The years it took to become a doctor."

Raymond gently knocked.

Mitchell peeked into the window. "I don't see any lights on."

He knocked harder.

The door swung open. "Come in!" Bren gestured.

Derek turned on the light as they entered.

While both men removed their coats, Russ sat up.

"This gentleman is my good friend, Dr. Mitchell Munson," Raymond said.

All greeted one another.

Raymond looked at Russ. "I thought you became a woman—"

"I way did earlier!"

Raymond appeared perplexed. "Boys, what's going on?"

"He was a woman but changed back into a man," Derek replied.

"You did?" Dr. Munson asked.

Russ nodded. "Like, totally."

"Unfortunately, he's back to his old self." Bren picked up his digital camera. "I snapped a few shots of him as a woman."

Raymond and Dr. Munson looked at the photo then simultaneously turned toward Russ.

He grinned, shrugging his shoulders.

"At least the photos are PG 13," Derek quipped.

Dr. Munson stepped back and cleared his throat. "Raymond informed me on the way down what had transpired. Evidently, all three of you had fallen into some type of liquid at a chemical plant. Then you, Russ, turned into a woman. Am I correct?"

"Like, you totally hit the mark, Doc."

Dr. Munson furrowed his eyebrows. "What did you say?"

"That's Russ' way of agreeing with you," Bren answered. "He has his own language."

"It took us a while to understand him," Derek added. "But, I'll translate if there's a problem."

Dr. Munson nodded. "Let me start out by telling you that I have heard about this very predicament when I was a mere boy growing up in Jamaica—"

"I thought you might think us to be disreputable," Bren interjected.

"Look who's totally got his own language now," Russ blurted out.

"So, you've heard about our situation?" Derek asked.

"Yes, my forefathers congregated around a campfire every night and told of stories they had heard or actually experienced," the doctor responded. "One particular night, an elder spoke about a unique tribe of people known as the Mayapo natives who lived deep deep in the jungle of the Amazon rainforest. Supposedly, they would change their prepubescent males into females for religious purposes and because of the procreative abilities of women. I did not think the story was true and thought it was just a crazy fable, but now I don't anymore. I cannot believe you experienced this same event."

"It's so crazy to majorly blow up like a chick," Russ stated.

"He said it was quite different turning into a woman," Derek remarked.

"I imagine the experience was disarming to say the least," Dr. Munson said.

"Like, I way dig your accent," Russ uttered. "It's totally dope."

"Would you speak with a better form of English?" Bren groused. "You can drop most of the adjectives and all your adverbs."

"I'm gonna majorly drop you in a minute," Russ touted.

Raymond stepped forward. "Guys, let Dr. Munson speak. After all, he's the one with a medical degree."

"Well, back in my good old Harvard days—"

"You went to Harvard?" Bren beamed.

"I was schooled in Jamaica and given the Hayward grant for my outstanding achievements in science," Dr. Munson replied. "From there, I went to Harvard."

"It's the most prestigious school on earth!" Bren gushed. "I'm quite impressed."

"With such high praise, I hope I do not disappoint you," Dr. Munson professed.

"Where'd you meet Raymond?" Derek asked.

"We worked a case together back in the day and have been close friends ever since," the doctor answered. He faced Raymond. "Do you remember it?"

"All too well," he admitted. "That was one of the hardest cases I've ever worked on. That is, up until now."

15

"It was quite the challenge." Dr. Munson agreed. "Well, I better get to work." He turned toward Russ. "Son, describe what you felt when you experienced the transformation."

"I was catching me some Z's when I felt this wicked cramping in my tummy." Russ rubbed his stomach. "Like, thinking some hurling was in my future, I tore into the bathroom and hugged the porcelain god feeling grody to the max. When nothing heaved, I felt a major quam furl from the noodle all the way down to my tootsies. I got up and totally gawked into the glass. Right before my eyes, I mutated into a major chick with jugs and a peach. It was crazy, dude."

Dr. Munson didn't say a word.

"I'll take this one!" Bren gestured. "Russ was sleeping. He became sick, started cramping, felt queasy all over and hated it. A sensation came over him, so he looked into the mirror and saw himself turn into a woman with breasts and a lady's nether region. It was quite overwhelming to see."

"I see," Dr. Munson finally spoke. "How much time did it take to complete your metamorphosis?"

"Like, one moment I'm majorly a dude then..." Russ snapped his fingers. "I'm a babe."

"I sort of understood what he just told me," the doctor said. "One moment you are a man and the next you are a woman."

"Welcome to Russ 101," Bren quipped.

"Well, he can joke all he wants. I'm shocked at the whole thing," Derek clamored. "I never thought it was humanly possible for a guy to turn into a girl—at least without surgery."

"It's unbelievable," Raymond decreed. "If I didn't know you guys, I'd say you were out of your minds, perhaps hallucinating on drugs or something of that sort. But I know you boys."

"Plus, the pictures on my camera," Bren added.

"Do you think that actual chemicals could've done this?" Derek asked.

Dr. Munson looked at him. "I feel they could—"

Russ began moaning as he clenched his stomach. Within seconds, he transformed into a woman.

16

Everyone gasped.

"Son, are you all right...I mean, Miss?" Dr. Munson's eyes had enlarged.

While the T-shirt fell to mid-thigh, Russ' boxer shorts hit the floor. "When the icky tummy cramps totally leave, I feel like me, but as a major girl," came the feminine voice.

The doctor shook his head. "Does it just happen?"

"Like, no," Russ replied in her altered tone. "I way took care of it myself."

"What do you mean?" Dr. Munson squinted.

"I totally shut my eyes and thought, 'I want to be a woman. I want to be a woman'...over and over again," she replied with a slight giggle. "Watch, I'll so turn back." Once her eyes closed, she thought hard. Seconds later, Russ was his manly self, pulling up his boxer shorts.

"Unbelievable!" Dr. Munson exclaimed. He took off his glasses and wiped them with a handkerchief. "When I sort this whole matter out, I will have to write a paper for the Journal of American Medicine."

Derek snickered. "That sounds neat and all, but what about us?"

"Have you two tried to turn into women?" Dr. Munson put his glasses back on and looked at both of them.

"No, I haven't," Derek replied.

"I don't want to try for fear I might become a woman and get stuck in that situation." Bren folded his arms. "I mean, what would I tell my parents? Hello, mom and dad, you have another twin daughter."

Derek smirked. "I just tried it but nothing happened."

"Like, the way I did it?" Russ queried.

"I closed my eyes and thought hard, 'I want to be a woman...I want to be a woman'...over and over again," Derek reacted.

"Maybe you did not get enough of the solution in your system or possibly you have not mastered the thought process," Dr. Munson said.

"If Russ was able to command this whole woman thing with his demented mind then it should be a cakewalk for both Derek and I," Bren remarked.

17

"Whoa dude, I'm in the room," came the reminder.

Bren looked at Russ. "You just go back to your thoughts about surfing and skateboarding while we grown-ups talk."

"You gentlemen will have to come with me to the hospital where I will conduct whatever tests are available to find out what is going on inside your bodies," Dr. Munson instructed. "It may be a long shot but I might just stumble upon something."

All three nodded.

"Did anybody get a sample of the solution you fell into?" Raymond asked.

"Yes, I did," Bren replied. "I wrung part of my wet shirt into a container I had in my duffle bag and sealed it."

Raymond nodded. "Great thinking!"

"Dr. Munson, can you have it analyzed for us?" Bren handed the sealed container to the doctor.

"I will drop it by the lab when we get to the hospital."

"Gather your belongings, guys," Raymond stated. "You'll ride with us to the hospital."

"I can drive," Bren noted. "It'll take my mind off our situation."

Raymond shook his head. "I don't think that's a good idea."

"We'll be fine," Derek added. "Besides, you don't like our taste in music."

"Listen, if you boys get into any trouble just honk the horn and for heaven's sake, stay close behind us," Raymond commented. "As a matter of fact, we'll follow you."

"Way cool! We can drag race," Russ quipped.

Bren sneered. "Only if we can drag you behind the car."

"C'mon guys, grab your stuff," Derek expressed. "It's a long ride, and my temper is quite short."

They shoved items into their bags and went to the car. Bren drove to the front office and dropped off the room key. He hopped back into the driver's seat and pulled out of the parking lot as Raymond followed in his Cadillac.

Without incidence, the guys discussed the case until they arrived at the hospital. Raymond passed them and pulled up to an adjacent building. The sign outside displayed the word MedLab as Dr. Munson entered. He came out a few minutes later and got back into the vehicle. Bren followed the Caddy as it entered the parking lot of the prestigious George Washington Hospital.

"Like, this place is totally rad," Russ commented.

Once Bren parked the car, they opened the doors, got out and went over to Dr. Munson. He was waving goodbye to Raymond who pulled away. All four walked in through the automated doors, entered into an elevator and got off on the second floor.

"Follow me, gentlemen."

Russ noticed the overhead sign that read: Infectious Disease. "Like, I hope we don't get some kind of grody infection."

Bren snickered. "You have enough problems with your female issues than to worry about catching anything else."

"Guys, play nice," Derek uttered. "We're all in a fragile state."

"Speak for yourself," Bren groused. "I feel quite stable."

After they passed the nurses' station, Dr. Munson turned a corner and went into a large room. "This is my office." He dropped his medical bag onto a large desk.

"Whoa, it's a totally mammoth room." Russ looked it over.

"The smarter the physician, the bigger the office!" Dr. Munson let out a hearty laugh. "I am just kidding, son. I head up the Infectious Disease department."

"Awesome," Derek stated. "We're in good hands."

"Yes, now follow me. You need to fill out the necessary paperwork." Dr. Munson walked out the door, down the hall and stopped at the receptionist's desk. "Becky, I need you to bring these gentlemen into exam room one and have each of them fill out the proper forms."

"Certainly."

"Is Cathy here?" he asked.

"Yes," Becky replied. "She's getting the sterilized instruments together that you called and requested for the examinations."

Dr. Munson turned toward the detectives. "I will see you gentlemen shortly." He walked away.

"Will you please come with me?" Becky picked up the clipboards with pens. "We'll go to exam room one. You can fill this out while you wait for the nurse." The men followed her to an enormous room housing an exam table, various trays with assorted implements and some heavy-duty equipment. A couple of sturdy lights hung from the ceiling, and there were some chairs against a wall. "Go ahead and have a seat." She handed each of them the proper forms. "Nurse Cathy will be in soon." The receptionist turned and left.

"Like, look at all that gnarly medical stuff," Russ uttered.

"You look at it." Bren shivered. "I hate physicals."

Derek's face rumpled. "Especially, the rump probe."

"Not me!" Russ filled in his form.

"That figures." Bren shook his head. "You're such a freak."

"And you're totally not?" Russ asked.

"Hardly," Bren replied.

Russ puffed. "Like, you're so vanilla—"

"And you're full of whipped cream and nuts," Bren countered.

"Knock it off, guys!" Derek chided. "Just complete your paperwork."

The door swung open. "Hello, my name is Cathy, and I'll be your nurse today." She carried in some items and placed them onto a tray. "I'll be back in a moment." She left and closed the door.

"Cool!" Russ exclaimed. "Like, she's majorly hot."

"There goes his hot fudge," Bren quipped.

The door opened again. This time, Dr. Munson came in. "I informed Cathy that I would not need her for the examinations."

"Aw, man," Russ muttered under his breath.

"Well, gentlemen, let us get to the bottom of this," Dr. Munson said. "Who wants to go first?"

"I'll totally do the dirty deed," Russ replied.

20

Dr. Munson took the clipboard and pen from him. "Son, your full name is Russ Munroe?"

"Like, totally, Doc."

"I will need you to change into a disposable gown." Dr. Munson went to a cabinet, pulled one out and handed it to him. "You can change behind the screen by the wall."

Russ sauntered toward it.

The doctor went up to Bren and Derek. "Gentlemen, I need your paperwork. They handed them over. "You can make yourselves comfortable in the waiting room across the hall."

"Like, no!" Russ rushed out from behind the screen with his clothes in hand. "They need to totally stay here for moral support."

"I wouldn't miss this for the world..." Bren smiled. "And trust me, he needs support for his morals or should I say his lack of them."

Derek nudged him and whispered, "Shut it."

Bren gave him a dirty look.

"I am fine with the three of you in here together, but you will have to fill out the required HIPAA forms before you leave," Dr. Munson said. "The hospital is a stickler when it comes to their rules."

Bren and Derek nodded.

Russ grinned. "So, where do I put my britches?" He looked around.

"Just put them on the chair you were sitting in." Dr. Munson pointed. "I will have you come over here so I can get your height and weight." He took a handheld recording device out of his lab coat, pushed a button, laid it down on the tray beside him and stood at the scale.

Russ swaggered over and hopped on it. "I went first because Bren is a major baby about getting a physical."

"You're the baby or should I say the brat," Bren countered.

Derek nudged him again.

"Like, no dude." Russ rubbed his soft features. "I've totally got a baby face."

"Well, shut your baby face!" Bren slid his chair away from Derek.

21

"Gentlemen, I am recording these examinations so they can be dictated afterwards." Dr. Munson warned. "I need all to be quiet."

They closed their mouths and sat up straight.

Dr. Munson held the recording device. "The patient is Russ Munroe," he said. "He is a twenty-three-year-old male presenting without symptoms. He is five-foot-nine and one hundred fifty pounds."

"Moo!" Bren jeered.

Russ smirked. "Like, you so weigh the same as me."

"Maybe, but I'm five-ten, fool." Bren shot back.

Russ huffed. "Derek is totally my height and weight."

"Whoa, how did I get dragged into this conversation?"

"Gentlemen, I am still recording this session," Dr. Munson repeated. He looked at Russ. "I need you to climb upon the exam table."

He jumped and his butt landed square in the center.

"Now son, to reiterate our earlier conversation. Last night you fell into a vat of liquid at a chemical company, and hours later you transformed into a woman." Dr. Munson intoned. "Is that correct?"

"Like, yeah, that's totally what happened." Russ watched the doctor wheel a machine over to him.

"I will explain everything as the examination progresses," Dr. Munson said. "If you have any questions, feel free to ask."

"I'm totally cool, Doc."

"First, the vital signs." Dr. Munson began. "I am putting a pulse ox on your finger. It will see how much oxygen is in your blood." At the same time, he popped a thermometer into Russ' mouth, grabbed his wrist and held it for a few seconds. "Your temperature is up, the pulse rate is rapid but your oxygen is steady—"

"Am I totally going to die?" Russ sounded alarmed.

"Yes, son," Dr. Munson reacted. "We all will someday," he added.

"Like, you way got me there," Russ chuckled.

22

Dr. Munson winked. "That is always an ice-breaker."

"You way broke mine into cubes," Russ uttered.

"Back to the drawing board," the good doctor said. "It is probably the chemicals in your body that are causing the disturbances. They are however mild, so we are tipping toward the plus side. I will now examine your head."

"I don't know why he's doing that," Bren stated. "There's nothing in there."

Derek leaned in. "Shut the hell up."

"You definitely need an anal probe." Bren sat back.

Dr. Munson ran his fingers throughout Russ' hair. "The scalp is free of nodules and adhesions. I will now take a look into your eyes. I need to use an ophthalmoscope for the exam." Light flicked into Russ' stare. "The pupils are equal, round, and reactive to light and accommodation." The doctor put the instrument down and picked up another. "This is an otoscope. I need you to open your mouth." He looked deep inside, flashed the beam into Russ' nose then went around to the ears. "The pharynx, gums, tongue, and roof of the mouth are free of granulomas. The nasal membrane is pink and the ear canal is unobstructed."

"I thought for sure he'd find some herpes sores," Bren whispered.

"Hush!" Derek huffed. "I want to hear this."

Dr. Munson pulled Russ' gown down to his waist and gently pushed his hands into various areas. "I am palpating the lymph nodes on both sides of the neck and the underarms. They are swollen." He took the stethoscope from around his neck and placed it on the patient's back. "Take a deep breath. Now breathe out. Take another deep breath. Breathe out." He placed the instrument back around his neck. "The lungs are clear to auscultation. The heart is rhythmic."

"I didn't think the doctor would've found a heart," Bren hissed. "With his attitude, I figured it was a lump of snot."

"Well, yours is made of stone," Derek countered. "Along with your hardened exterior."

Dr. Munson rubbed Russ' chest. "The breasts are free of cysts and nodulations. Now son, I need you to lie flat on your back."

"Ok, Doc."

23

The good doctor extended the examination table. He palpated the areas around Russ' upper and lower abdomen, liver, kidneys, pancreas, spleen and finally the appendix. "There is an absence of hernias," he spoke. "I now need you to lie on your left side. I have to do a rectal exam."

Derek's butt cheeks cringed.

"God knows what he'll find up inside there," Bren commented.

Dr. Munson reached under Russ' hospital gown with his moistened finger.

"Whoa, dude!" Russ reared up from the examination table. "Like, why is it totally wet?"

"Son, it's petroleum jelly," Dr. Munson replied.

"It's so slithery," Russ announced.

Derek pointed his finger in Bren's face. "Don't say it."

"What?" He smiled.

"Exactly!" Derek smirked.

"The prostate is smaller than normal," Dr. Munson observed.

"Like, what does that mean?" Russ looked bummed out.

"I won't know until all the results come back," Dr. Munson answered. "This will include lab work that will be drawn after the examination." He took off the used glove and put on a fresh one. "I need you to lie on your back again."

Russ rolled over as the doctor lifted up the bottom of the gown. He checked out the genitals. "The lymph nodes in the groin are swollen. The scrotum is eased and the testes are free from cysts or nodulations. The penis is circumcised. You are a healthy young man."

Russ chuckled. "That's what the babes majorly tell me."

Dr. Munson checked the legs for swelling, searched for a pulse in the knee and foot then observed the joints and muscles. "I need you to sit up." He pushed the gown up high on Russ' thighs. "I have to check your reflexes." He hit them with a small hammer and they jerked forward.

"That felt totally weird."

24

"You need to stand up so I can check out the alignment of your legs and the straightness of your back," Dr. Munson said. "Now ambulate so I can watch your gait."

"Like, what?"

"You need to walk, son," he replied. "I need to make sure you are walking normally."

Russ strutted around the room with his usual swagger.

"The last test is neurological," Dr. Munson noted. "Give me your hands. Now squeeze. Hop on one foot. Now the other. And bend your legs. Good. Now do me the courtesy and turn yourself into a woman."

"That'll be way easy." Russ closed his eyes. He clutched his stomach and moaned. A moment later, he morphed into a female."

The doctor stood in awe then shook his head. "Sorry about that. I have never seen this before and feel enamored by the situation."

"That's way cool," she uttered. "I am totally hot."

Bren looked at Derek as they rolled their eyes.

"Please, follow me over to this other examination table." Dr. Munson pointed. "I have to put you in stirrups."

"Like, the ones that are on a mechanical bull...giddy-up!"

The doctor smiled. "Similar mechanics, different tool."

She giggled.

As Dr. Munson completed the thorough examination, his patient changed back into a man. "You will be sent downstairs for a full work-up of blood tests. Stat, of course. I am also ordering an EEG, an EKG, a chest X-ray, and both CT and MRI scans with and without contrast. They will check for any abnormalities that could be throughout your body. First, this will be done while you are a man. Next, you will turn into a woman and have the same results done again. My nurse, Cathy, will be with you the entire time as a liaison. She is aware of your situation and will put you under an assumed name. No one will be the wiser. Do you have any questions?"

"Like, I don't know what you just said, but it's cool with me." Russ leaped off the table.

"Careful, son!" Dr. Munson cautioned.

25

"I'm totally rough and tumble, Doc."

"But still not unbreakable," the doctor maintained.

Russ sauntered over to the chair, threw off his gown and began to put his boxers on.

"Must you do that right here?" Bren snarled. "Take it behind the screen." His hand gestured. "Nobody wants to see any of that."

"Chicks majorly do." Russ grinned.

Bren smirked. "Do you see any here?"

"Not yet, but you two could totally turn into one that fast." Russ snapped his fingers.

Bren looked away.

"Which one of you gentlemen is next?" Dr. Munson asked.

Bren pointed. "Take him."

"Really?" Derek snickered as he got up.

Dr. Munson laughed. "I save my best exam for last." He vigorously rubbed his hands together.

Bren's expression resembled a little boy who got caught with his hand in the cookie jar.

When the examinations and relative tests were completed, Dr. Munson had the guys go to lunch in the hospital cafeteria. He instructed them to return and have a seat in his waiting room when they finished.

After eating, all three felt tired. They trudged back and plopped down into a chair. The weariness showed on their faces.

A door finally opened. "Gentlemen, come into my office." The doctor invited them.

"You have our results?" Derek queried.

"Yes, but first, I need to call your boss." Dr. Munson sat behind his desk, picked up the phone and dialed. "Hello, Raymond, it's Mitchell. I have your fellas with me. The phone is now on speaker."

"Hey guys, how are you all feeling?" Raymond asked.

"I'm ready to hit the hay and crash," Derek retorted.

Dr. Munson picked up his paperwork. "I wanted everyone to hear what I have to say together. This way, there will be no misinformation traveling about."

"I appreciate that," Raymond said.

"I want to start out by saying that when Russ was a woman, she had all the usual female organs," the doctor continued. "A fully formed vagina, a uterus, cervix, ovaries; you get the picture. The rest of my findings however are a mixed bag. Many of the complete blood counts, chemistry screens, metabolic panels and urinalysis came back somewhat abnormal."

"What does that mean?" Bren enquired.

"I will forego the medical mumbo-jumbo and put it into a language you can understand," Dr. Munson responded. "Let us start with the endocrine system. Its job is to send information from one set of cells to another. It instructs the release of approximately twenty chemicals inside of your bodies at any given time. What I am basically saying is your hormones are askew. It seems that your thyroid gland, which is considered the master gland, is the biggest culprit. The numbers are completely off the charts. The two lobes are usually shaped like butterfly wings but now they are shaped more like bird wings, and I am not referring to a hummingbird."

"Whoa!" Derek released.

"Next, your adrenal glands which are located on the kidneys are not producing adequately. They are quite out of kilter," the doctor revealed. "Then we have the hypothalamus. This very important gland is usually the size of a pearl but inside each of your boys it is at least the size of a large marble or what I called back in my day, a steely."

Russ beamed. "Like, I totally played with them too."

"We're all thrilled." Bren rolled his eyes.

"So it's about the size of a golf ball," Derek remarked.

"That is a better reference for the pineal gland which is found in the brain and usually about the size of a pea. The secretion from this gland starts the onset of puberty. Your pineal gland is close to ten times the normal size along with your pituitary glands," Dr. Munson stated. "All of this information combined could be what has

27

transformed Russ from a male into a female. Of course, this is just a hypothesis but I feel the solution you fell into is the culprit."

"How could some liquid cause this to happen?" Derek questioned.

"Well, son, whatever the ingredients, they were potent enough to interfere with your hormones and other important bodily fluids," Dr. Munson answered. "Something inside of me is saying that this solution is not a man-made or synthetic compound. It has an organic feel to it."

"You mean, something natural could've done this?" Bren declared.

If scientists can kill certain cancer cells in a laboratory with the bark of a Mounge tree, who knows what else is growing out there and being harvested?" Dr. Munson shrugged. "When I was a very young boy, my grandmother would brew what she called 'remedies' for any ailment you had. Whether it was a bad cold, a skin condition or whatever ailment one had, she could cure them. I would call it the 'fix mix'. Everything she used came out of a nearby forest. Some items smelled like the dickens and others, they looked like they had grown on another planet—"

The telephone beeped. "Raymond, let me put you on hold a moment. My other line is blinking."

"Go ahead."

"Hello, this is Dr. Munson." He picked up a pen, jotted down some information and switched off the hold button. "Raymond, are you there?"

"Yes, I'm here."

"I told the lab to run the solution Stat and they actually did," the doctor commented. "Other than the associated chemicals from the shirt, they isolated five individual compounds. However, one is posing a problem and as I expected, it is of a natural origin and therein lays our dilemma—"

"Wait a minute!" Raymond cried. "We have all of them."

"What?" Dr. Munson asked.

Bren slapped a palm against his forehead. "Oh, you know I'm tired," he bellowed. "We were already given the names of these man-made and natural substances."

28

"Duh!" Derek edged forward in his chair. "How could we have forgotten that?

Russ grinned. "Like, this is what your brain totally looks like on drugs!"

"Am I going to be let in on this?" Dr. Munson beckoned.

"Mitchell, the case we're currently working on involves this formula," Raymond replied. "We were given the names and descriptions of each ingredient. It never dawned on me. I will fax it to you. Let me know what you think of them?"

"My grandmother taught my mother all of her mixtures so I will mail her a copy to see if she recognizes any of them," Dr. Munson uttered. "I will also talk with my aunt in Jamaica to see if there is anything organic she might know of that could do something to this degree. There are a lot of homeopathic remedies still foreign to the United States that I might be able to use to counteract the recurring imbalances in the numbers thus stabilizing their bodies. Sometimes natural can fight natural without all those pesky side effects."

"I just hope your family can depress, repress or suppress our female sides with their remedies," Bren stated.

"Like, is that voodoo?" Russ' eyes became as wide as saucers.

Dr. Munson smiled. "It is now referred to as Black Magic."

"I don't care what color it is, as long as it helps us," Derek remarked.

"What about hormones?" Bren brought up.

Dr. Munson shook his head. "They could do more harm than good. It would be extremely difficult to get the dosing correct with multiple hormones. It is not an exact science, even with test results. Plus, imbalances can cause sterility, strokes, heart attacks, gynecomastia, testicular shrinkage, blood clots, cancer, baldness"

"Baldness!" Russ clamored. "Like, there's no way I'm majorly losing my hair." He swung his head from side to side.

"Oh, please," Bren snarled. "You could lose half that mop and still have plenty enough to scour the floor."

Russ stopped, allowing the blonde curls to fall against his shoulders. "I'd totally be a woman first."

29

"Gentlemen," the doctor interrupted. "Do not worry about the hormones at this time. Instead, I want to keep you overnight and let some other specialists look at you."

"Not me!" Bren protested.

"No way," Derek quipped. "I'm not being guinea-pigged on."

"Like, me either."

"Well, I guess that is definitely out of the question," Dr. Munson uttered. "If you gentlemen should get worse, I want to be contacted immediately."

"I will make sure, Mitchell," Raymond decreed.

"Gentlemen, you are sleep deprived, and all this information is quite taxing on the mind," the doctor stated. "You should go home and get some rest. It cures a multitude of sins."

"Boys, come on home," Raymond urged. "You three need to sleep."

They got up from their chairs.

"Raymond, I will call you later. Good day." Dr. Munson hung up. He rose from his chair and walked around the desk. "Gentlemen, call me at any time, for any reason, even if it is just to talk. I am here for you."

"Thank you," each of them expressed. After saying their goodbyes, they left and went straight home to snooze.

Chapter 3

Lydia Reome entered through the gates of the palatial Algonquin Estates, a 50-story complex that towered over the cityscape. It touted indoor shopping and underground parking for its indulged residents.

After pulling into a 'visitors-only' parking spot, she got out of her car and walked into the building. A security guard was seated behind a huge desk.

"Hello!" Lydia smiled.

He stood. "May I help you?"

"I am here to see Mr. Logan Price."

"The Speaker of the House," the security guard noted.

She reacted to his warmth. "Yes, please."

"May I see your driver's license?"

"I have it right here." Lydia rummaged through her Gucci handbag and retrieved a matching wallet. She opened the clasp and handed it to him.

"You are French?"

"Oui." She smiled.

The guard grinned. "I thought I recognized the accent," he said. "How long will you be in Washington, DC?"

"Just a few days," she replied. "But, I hope after this week it will be permanent."

"It's a great place to live." He handed her wallet back. "Mr. Price is on the forty-fourth floor, otherwise known as the penthouse suite."

"What is his suite number? Lydia asked.

"He owns the entire forty-fourth floor."

Her eyes expanded. "Thank you very much!" She jammed the wallet back into her purse.

"The elevators are behind me and to the left." The guard pointed. 'Bring this to the attendant and he will take you up. Have a good night."

"I intend to." She winked at him. "Goodbye."

Lydia went over to the elevator attendant and handed him an item. Both got on. He inserted a strange-looking key then turned it. With the push of a button, they headed toward the penthouse suite. *I would love to live like this, as the wife of the Speaker of the House. This night has to go well.* It stopped and opened to a sitting area with a make-up mirror. After flashing a quick smile, she got out, went over and looked into it. *Oh, how dreadful! I need to fix my face and fluff up this hair.* After doing so, she reached out and rang the doorbell. Seconds later, she heard a rustling at the door and saw a shadow pass the peephole.

"Who is it?"

"It is Lydia Reome."

Logan opened the door and escorted her in. "How're you today?"

"I am good." She greeted him by placing her lips to his. "And you?"

"Great, now that you're here." He reached his hand out. "May I take your coat?"

"Please." She slipped it off.

He took it from her and hung it on the coat rack. "How did your lecture go?"

"It went well. Only half the room fell asleep."

"Not with such a gorgeous speaker to look at." He stroked her back.

"You would be surprised." She stepped down into the living room. "But, thank you."

He grinned. "How was the drive down?"

"That was not so good." Lydia walked toward the balcony. "How do you deal with all the traffic?"

"I have a driver," Logan replied. "Being the Speaker of the House does have its perks."

"Where do I sign up for that job?" She approached the sliding glass doors.

"Sorry, baby, it's already taken, but a vacancy could be a mere step away."

She gazed out as dots of light shimmered across the city. "Are you asking me to stick around?"

"Isn't that a great view?" He wrapped his arm around her waist. "I enjoy watching the dusk roll in."

"It is quite beautiful," she added. "You can see all of Washington, DC from here."

"That's how I keep my eye on everything." He pulled her closer.

"You are so silly." She broke free and maneuvered around him.

"Getting back to sticking around, are you?"

"I thought you were avoiding the issue."

"Why would I do that?"

Lydia leaned in and kissed him. "Would you be so kind as to show me the rest of your home?"

"Follow me..." Logan clasped his hand around hers. "Each room has an entrance to the next. It's all in a full circle."

"I just adore big, round things."

"Then we shouldn't have any problems."

She giggled as he toured her around. When finished, they ended up in the kitchen. He turned toward her and let his hand drop to her hip.

"Would you care for a glass of wine?"

"That would be great." She brushed by his forearm.

"Red or white?"

"Whatever you want is fine with me." She winked. "I am French. I love them all."

"Oui!"

"Parlez-vous Francais?"

"Um—"

"Do you speak French?"

"No, not at all."

She leaned against the spacious island. "I will have to teach you."

He grinned. "Just the French kissing part."

"Our first lesson will begin after dinner."

"Then I better get cooking."

"Oui!"

"I picked up a 2009 Chateau Lafite Rothschild."

She purred. "Ooh, delicious."

"We can have a glass now, and the rest with dinner."

"What are we having?"

"I've been craving spaghetti and meatballs all week." He popped out the cork. "I picked up some Italian bread at a swanky bakery in Barbour Square. There're some really nice restaurants in that district. We'll go there one night."

"My mouth is watering at the thought."

"Then here..." Logan handed her a glass of wine. "Dry them with this."

Lydia grasped the stem and took a sip. "Ooh, it is delicious."

"It's not the only thing that is." He winked at her.

She smiled. "This is the only thing that I am going to taste at the moment."

"Is that so?" He inched closer.

She thrust out her hand.

"So, you're keeping me at bay?"

34

"Just for the moment," Lydia replied. "I am hungry and want to eat."

Logan's eyebrow arched. "That was my plan too."

"You are so bad."

"And at the same time so good." He backed away.

She dropped her hand to the wineglass, picked it up and took another sip.

"Would you care to make a salad?"

"I relish the idea."

"Everything's in the refrigerator." He opened the door. "Down in the vegetable bin."

She bent down.

"Ahem, while you're down there—"

"Logan!" Lydia looked up.

"I was going to ask you to pick out a salad dressing." He grinned. "They're on the door at the bottom."

"Why do I feel you are up to something?"

His hand hung on the door. "Only part of me is."

She shook her head and looked back down. "Your refrigerator is so neat and orderly."

"That's me, neat freak central."

"I really like cleanliness." She got up. "It is sort of sexy."

"Wow, if you think that's sexy..." He turned and pointed. "Go look in my cupboards. You'll be all hot and bothered."

She opened a couple of doors. "Oh, my goodness! Everything has its place and stocked so perfectly, I might add."

"You may definitely add." He stepped closer to her.

She slung her arms around his shoulders and kissed him on the lips. He pulled her tight as she placed a hand against his chest. "That is your first French lesson."

"I can't wait until my second!"

Lydia pulled away. "I need a drink."

35

"Me, too." Logan grabbed the wine bottle. He brought it to his lips and gulped down a mouthful.

"Before you finish it, will you top off my glass?"

"Your wish is my command!"

"Then we will not have any problems."

"None whatsoever." He put down the empty bottle.

"My first wish would be a knife..." She smiled. "While the lettuce is still firm."

"That's not all that's firm." He grinned. "It's in the top drawer on the right side of the stove."

"Merci!" Lydia turned, opened the drawer and pulled out a huge knife. "This should do the job."

Logan ran water into a large pot and placed it atop of the stove then turned on the burner. "The smaller ones are in the next drawer over."

"My mother always told me—the bigger the tool—the better the results." She winked.

He winked back. "Well, I don't want to argue with your mother, but they're not always right."

She leaned in. "Most of the time they are."

"You win." He quickly snuck a kiss.

She snapped her head back. "I always do."

"You always will with me."

She slammed the knife into the lettuce, splitting it in half. "You are a smart man."

"I know." He nodded. "My mother taught me well."

"She did." Lydia eased a piece of lettuce into her parted lips. "Where is the salad bowl?"

Logan pointed behind her. "It's on the bottom of that wine rack."

She sashayed over and spotted a bottle of wine. "I see you drink Pouilly-Fuisse?"

"I do," he replied. "It's great with seafood."

She picked it up. "Yes, I know."

"You like it too?"

"I love it!" She put it back down.

"We should have it with dinner." He turned around and grabbed a bottle opener from the drawer. "Bring it to me and I'll open it. I want it to breathe."

"Just one glass with dinner." She handed it to him. "I need to stay alert for our get-together tonight. I have to make a first good impression."

"I wanted to speak to you about that." He slid out the cork. "We moved the meeting to tomorrow night. Also, the location has changed for the reformulation, but our plan remains the same."

"I do not understand." Lydia turned away from the cutting board.

"Last night, we were at Henry's business having a meeting when a friend called to inform me that the local police were setting up roadblocks on either side of the building. I was also told that the FBI were on their way."

"What did you do?"

"Well, I couldn't be seen at Prescott Chemicals," Logan retorted. "I mean, what business does the Secretary of State have with the owner of a chemical plant, and so late at night?" He shrugged. "Let alone in the company of a chemist and the leader of a militia group, who've been a thorn in the government's paw with their claims of dirty back door deals with corrupt men who fill the halls of Congress."

"How did you all get out of there?"

"I got out by traveling down an old dirt path behind Prescott Chemicals. It took me forever in a day to get to the other side of his twenty-seven-acre property," he groused.

"What happened to the others?"

"All three were taken to the FBI's interrogation rooms for most of the night. I got them out as soon as I could with the help of another friend."

37

"Do you know the trouble you could have brought on yourself if found with those men?" Lydia shook her head. "You would have kissed the Presidency goodbye!"

"Don't remind me," Logan remarked. "I'd rather get a kiss from you." His lips puckered up.

She gave him a quick smooch. "Where is the new location?"

"It's in an old underground bomb shelter behind an even older farmhouse."

"Is that where I will be reformulating the formula?"

"Yes, you and Buford will work on it together. Only he's under the impression that you'll be taking cues from him."

"That will never happen," Lydia hissed. "I made a promise to myself that I would never be second chair to another man. All they do is try to impress you with their knowledge as if I am not smart enough to understand it." Her eyes glared. "Not only did I know it, but I was way ahead of him from the beginning."

"Honey, you cannot makes waves with Buford." Logan cajoled her. "He and Henry go back years and if there's going to be friction then you'll be the one they'd let go and this plan would've been for nothing."

She huffed. "Men—you are all alike!"

"No, I'm different!" He wrapped his arms around and coddled her. "I know this goes against everything you stand for..." He dropped the embrace and stared into her eyes, his voice dropped to nearly a whisper. "I really need your help."

She sighed. "I will do this for the both of us."

"Good." Logan turned and stirred in the spaghetti. "Henry Prescott will offer you a position at his chemical company tomorrow night. We are meeting him at the Back Alley Bar. Remember our little pillow talk at the hotel?"

"Vividly!" She diced a tomato.

"Then you recall that I told you what the initials M.A.G.O.C. stood for, and how we're a militia group that's watching our government's every move."

"Yes."

38

"I didn't tell him about our entire conversation. I might've left out the fact that I shared intimate details about...well, everything. I mean, he wasn't told about your knowledge of the inner workings of the organization or how you already know what TB4711 stands for. Henry has no clue that I told you what our intentions are so you cannot slip up or allude to anything I've told you. Just act surprised."

"I am a very good actress when it comes to men." She sliced down the center of a cucumber. "I have the ability to emote any emotion at any time I see fit."

He stirred the spaghetti. "So, am I any man?"

"No!" She turned around to look at him. "You are currently the man."

His eyes squinted.

"I meant to say, the man I am dating."

"Oh."

"Do not worry."

"When somebody says that, it's time to worry."

She put down the knife and held his hand. "You misunderstood me."

"Then elaborate," he said. "What did you mean?"

"Men run this world," she replied. "Women have to compete with them just to be heard, and a university-educated woman has to shout the loudest. We must don many hats when dealing with a man's various moods. If one does not become a good actress then she is consigned to the back of the line, never to be received."

"Just so you know, I hear you loud and clear."

"Now you know why you are my man."

He hugged her then his hand moved south.

"That hat is off for the moment."

He let go.

Lydia turned back around and picked up the knife "So, you were telling me about Mr. Prescott."

"Henry will tell you that the formula his company is manufacturing needs to be perfected, and you will be working with his lead chemist on the project." He turned off the burner. "Everything will be on a need to know as you go basis. Your task is to take the job."

"How do they expect me to perfect something that I know hardly anything about?" She cut into an onion.

"Eventually, you'll know everything." He took a jar of spaghetti sauce out of the cabinet and removed the lid. "Henry will think that by then you're in too deep and will not inform the authorities. Plus, he'll offer you some to use at your discretion as a way to buy your silence."

"Which I would certainly take!" She picked up her wineglass and took a sip. "I have somebody in mind that needs to be formulized." She smirked. "Before Mr. Prescott has second thoughts, I will transfer some into an empty perfume bottle and mark it 'personal use only'."

Logan grabbed a colander and placed it into the sink. "Only after our mission is completed."

Lydia took another sip then put it down. "Of course, dear."

"And for heaven's sakes..." He drained the pot. "Don't get caught."

"I am as sly as a fox."

He grinned. "Well, come here, foxy, and give me a growl."

She slinked up and snarled at him.

"Ooh, I'll be your wolf." He howled. "I'm ready to mate!"

"You need to control that animal magnetism because your sauce is bubbling."

He looked down.

She pointed. "The one on the stove."

He spun around, grasped the large spoon and started stirring.

"So, who is this person working on the formula that I am supposed to assist?"

40

"His name is Buford Higgins." The stirring continued. "He's the only one who's allowed near it."

Lydia stroked the back of his neck. "I do not need him."

"I know, but he needs you!" Logan turned around. "Listen, he's the lead chemist on this, not to mention he co-discovered the original solution," he pleaded. "Buford needs to think that he perfected this concoction, so please, tell me you'll cooperate with him?"

She placed her hands on his chest. "Whatever you wish, I will do."

"Thanks, baby." He squeezed her closer.

"You now know you owe me big." She smiled. "Really big."

"Oh, I know."

"I need to finish the salad." She tried to writhe from his clutches.

"Who's stopping you?" He let go.

Lydia smirked then turned toward the cutting board and gripped the knife. She picked up a stalk of celery and began chopping.

Logan came up from behind. "You cut that celery so delicately." He nibbled her ear.

She wriggled. "I am chopping!"

"Make sure they're in small chunks."

"I will chop you into small chunks if you do not stir that bubbling spaghetti sauce." She pointed the knife in the oven's direction.

He swirled the sauce with a large spoon then edged up and again grasped her. "Could you finely shred the carrots?" His warm breath tickled the side of her face.

"I am going to shred you in a moment if you do not let go."

"I might like that—"

"Oh, you would, but our dinner will become cold in the meantime and I am famished."

"I'm also hungry, but not for food." He moved his hands over her shoulders.

"Put your hands on the meatballs and cook them," she ordered. "Or I will starve you from everything."

41

"Wow, are you threatening me already with that?" He opened the freezer.

"Not yet!" Lydia snatched a single white candle from the end of the counter. "But, I will if you do not prepare them."

"They only need to be nuked." He took off the lid. Logan popped them inside the microwave, closed the door and pushed a button.

"I want them hot." She enunciated each word.

"Oh, they'll sizzle." He advanced toward her.

After reaching into her purse, she pulled out a pack of matches, lit one and held it up. "Back...or something will be seared."

"Ooh, foreplay."

She lit the candle as the microwave beeped.

"Saved by the bell," came her utterance.

Logan smirked at her then took out the meatballs. "Wow, look at the steam," he said. "I'm exuding that much also."

"Then come here." Lydia opened the refrigerator door. "This should cool you down." She nudged by him, collected the remaining items, put them in and closed it.

"The bedroom would've been better."

"And how do you figure?"

"The door has been closed for a while and I left the window open." He grinned. "That would cool things down."

"Maybe for the moment." She edged closer to him. "But, with us in there, it would become hotter than in this kitchen."

"What's wrong with a little heat?" He touched the arch of her back.

"Nothing!" She smiled. "I love being hot. It is the French in me."

"Oh, now you're just tormenting me." He pulled her close against him.

"Why would I do that?"

"Because you can."

She pressed her lips against his and passionately kissed him.

42

"What about a little dessert before dinner?" He tightened his grasp.

"I guess a tad would not hurt." She gazed into his eyes.

"I want more than that."

Her eyebrow arched. "I have to watch my waistline."

"By the time I'm finished, you'll lose an inch."

"You might also."

"Baby, spare me my inch. I need all I have, especially with a French woman."

She jumped up and wrapped her legs around his waist. "European women spare nothing."

They slammed into the refrigerator door. Logan swung her around and headed toward the bedroom. As he furiously grasped for the doorknob, Lydia clung to him, plunging her lips into his. He flung open the door, staggered to the bed and dropped onto the plush comforter while clawing at her. They ripped off clothes. A shirt flew here, a blouse flew there. Pants were hurled here, a skirt soared there. Before they knew it, the sheets became entangled between them as luscious lips led into ferocious foreplay.

"Wait, please," she blurted out while jerking her head to the side.

"What's the matter?" he asked, huffing and puffing.

She tucked her tousled hair behind both ears. "The last time we did this...well, I was drunk."

"I was too." He shrugged. "So what?"

"Everything happened so fast." She slid out from beneath him. "I barely remember a thing."

"You were really good if that's what you're worried about."

"That is not the issue."

"Then what?" He budged alongside her. "Am I moving too fast?"

"No, it is not you..." She hesitated. "It is me."

"What do you mean?"

She exhaled.

"Is this the brush-off?"

43

"No!"

"Then what is it, baby?" His eyes drooped.

"It is just that I jump in so fast when it comes to men." Her lips pouted. "That is why my relationships fall apart. I do not get to know a person. I just want to kiss and talk, and get to know you better. I want it to be different this time. I am looking for something that will last."

"Is that all?" He slid his arm around her. "We'll get to know each other. I promise. Now let's kiss for a while, and then we'll talk."

"No!" Lydia pushed his face away with the palm of her hand. "Let us talk then maybe we will kiss."

"Ok, you want to get to know me." Logan leaned on his elbow. "I'm five-eight with a five-eleven personality." He pointed to the top of his head at his receding hairline. "This has no personality."

She laughed. "You are so funny."

"No, my appearance is funny," he said. "I wish I looked like Brad Pitt instead of a pit bull."

"Do not make fun of yourself." She turned onto her side. "You look nice and need to represent it."

"You can say that looking like Angelina Jolie." He shook his head. "I wasn't afforded the luxury of good looks."

"Stop! I mean it." She rubbed his arm. "You are cute."

"As a bug's ear."

Lydia ignored his comment. "Not to mention you are a very important man at a very important place—the White House," she said in an effort to build up his ego.

"I'm the third man from the presidency. Big deal."

She slapped him on the arm. "That is not representing!"

"No, it's reprehensible."

"Do not say that." She slapped him again.

He grabbed her and kissed her.

Lydia pulled away. "Logan—"

"What?"

44

"Tell me what is inside you?" She stared into his eyes. "What makes Logan Price tick?"

"Well, I'm ambitious, and don't care who or what bodies I have to step over to be the President of the United States."

"Now that is what I am talking about." She egged him on. "What else?"

"I'm just biding my time until I can take the Grand Seat."

"I like a go-getter!" She prodded him on.

"I learned at boarding school that you've got to take what you want. I majored in economics with a minor in political science which taught me to use everybody and everything to get where I'm at today. I went from a mayor to a governor then into the senate seat until where I am now. Bold moves are what you need."

"Now that is a representative."

Logan's stomach gurgled. "I'm starving."

"I am also quite hungry."

"Are we still starting with dessert?"

"Bon appetite!"

Lydia slinked on top of Logan, stretched out a leg and switched off the light with a sweep of her toes.

45

Chapter 4

The mid-morning sun lingered high above while its pleasant rays penetrated the three-bedroom loft over the Davenport Detective Agency. The kitchen was filled with stainless steel appliances and opened onto an adjoining dining room that held an ultramodern glass table with four satin-finished black metal chairs. The living room, which bordered both areas, contained a posh grey-twilled sofa with two matching chairs placed at opposite ends. An assortment of throw pillows dispensed color against pastel walls as the end tables basked their dark hues on a richly-textured carpet.

In the middle of the furniture sat an elongated coffee table with a spread of male-oriented magazines and the TV Guide. A large-screen television was mounted on the wall across the room for maximum viewing pleasure. A curio cabinet housing various knick-knacks and treasured trinkets the guys had collected from the many cases they had cracked stood on an adjacent wall.

While Derek napped on the couch, Russ stood in the kitchen with the refrigerator door open. Bren entered the living room wearing a pair of Ralph Lauren boxer shorts.

"It's toasty in here."

"Like, totally." Russ turned his head. "Nice hanging horse."

Bren spun around and looked down. "Where, I don't see it?"

Russ chuckled. "Like, that's what she said!"

"You're an idiot," Bren bellowed.

"I was way talking about the little Polo horse on the side of your boxers, dude." Russ looked back into the fridge. "You never walk around in your bloomers, so I totally haven't seen the logo before."

"Well, I happen to be very warm," Bren stated. "My body always runs a degree or two higher. Even at Dr. Munson's office, it was 99.8."

"Like, hot blood—cold heart," Russ mumbled.

"Are you going to just stand there and let all of the cold air out?" Bren asked. "You have been staring into that refrigerator for the last five minutes."

"I'm totally parched and so need something to way quench it."

"Then let me make you my famous cocktail over ice," Bren offered. "I promise you, it's quite refreshing and will quell your thirst—"

"And all other bodily functions..." Derek sat up. "It's two parts hemlock to one part cyanide with a splash of arsenic."

"You need to roll back over and finish your nap," Bren barked.

Derek kicked off the covers. "Who can sleep with you two going at it?" He picked up some type of equipment and put an object into his ear.

"Like, what's he doing?"

Bren shrugged. "It's probably one of his electronic contraptions—"

"Shhh..." Derek let out.

"Who's he shushing?" Bren whispered.

Russ smirked. "I'd totally say us."

"Thanks, I wouldn't have guessed that one." Bren jeered.

Both watched Derek push buttons and move dials. Once finished, it was laid back down on the end table. He edged off the couch, pulled his jeans on, got up and stretched.

"What was that all about?" Bren asked.

Derek put his arms down. "You're just dying to know."

"I'll be dead soon if you don't hurry up" Bren uttered.

"Ok, take a chill pill," Derek quipped. "What the two of you were enthralled with is a little something I finagled from one of my many sites. When we were at Prescott Chemicals, I planted a voice-activated audio recorder on the back of the computer—"

47

"Like, totally cool, dude!"

Derek grinned. "It's really awesome to hear what I've captured so far."

"I want to listen to it," Bren clamored.

"Hold on, I'll put it on speaker so you both can admire my work." Derek turned and pressed a button. "Here we go!"

"I informed Dave McNally to shut down all operations until sometime next week. Everyone will get their paychecks. Tell them it's a paid vacation," Henry said as his voice became louder with every step. "My receptionist, Nadine, will do the same with the cleaning crew. Most of them are her relatives anyways."

"I told you I'd take care of things," Logan crowed.

"I'm just glad your lawyer friend came and got us out of the interrogation rooms when he did," Henry stated. "After ten hours of constant bombardment from angry officials, I was getting nervous that Arvin or Buford would cut a deal."

"I bet you were glad when Jameson Bradshaw rescued you."

"You've got that right," Henry declared. "He seemed awful young to be a lawyer."

"His father is Samuel Bradshaw of the prestigious law firm of Bradshaw, Ellsworth and Sinclair," Logan articulated. "Old-fashioned blackmail got you out."

"I guess I'm missing your point."

"The point being that it was free," Logan proclaimed. "I had photos of him at the Atrium Hotel in some compromising positions with a male hustler. Once I knew you were out and dropped off at your homes, they were sent to his office in a brown envelop marked fragile. I added a little note saying he wouldn't want the new bride finding out about his proclivities."

"Would you tell me again why were friends?"

"Oh, don't forget about our meeting at the Back Alley Bar tonight," Logan stressed. "Lydia is in town. She arrived late yesterday. Since the location has been altered, we'll need her more than ever."

48

"That reminds me, I've got to pick up Buford soon," Henry noted. "We're going over to Milford County to get the equipment for our expensive project—"

"You will be paid handsomely so I wouldn't bicker if I were you," Logan issued.

"I'd love to rip that heap of junk out of the wall and bring it to the bunker..." His voice grew much louder. "Unfortunately, if the authorities came back and found it missing, they'd know something was up and be up our asses."

"Then leave it behind," Logan urged. "I need to head back to DC and see if there's any news about...well, anything. If Lydia takes this position, she'll most likely live with me."

"As long as we get this formula done and soon, I could care less if she lived in the White House," Henry said as his vocals began fading.

"Now that's the spirit..." Logan's voice trailed off.

Derek clicked it off.

Russ snickered. "Whoa, those dudes are back at it—"

"Just not at Prescott Chemicals," Derek interjected.

"We'll have to find out their new location," Bren uttered. "But first, we need to conjure up a plan for our stakeout tonight."

Russ took out a carton of orange juice and closed the fridge door. "I'm so opening a window to let in some air flow."

Derek nodded. "Sounds cool to me."

"Don't let any bugs in," Bren shrieked.

Russ scoffed. "I'll totally swat them down, just like I'll do to you if that grody trap of yours doesn't slam shut."

Bren snarled. "Give it your best shot."

"Guys, knock it off," Derek snapped.

"That was my plan," Bren asserted.

"Not a good one." Derek tossed the folded blanket on the back of the couch. "Russ would've beaten you to a pulp."

"Speaking of pulp..." Russ burped. "Like, we're totally out of OJ" He tipped the carton back and swilled the last drops into his mouth.

"Would you please use a glass?" Bren insisted. "Nobody wants to catch your venereal diseases."

Russ dropped the container and clutched his stomach. "Like, dudes, these cramps are grody!" He doubled over. "Ouch, ah man!" His voice wobbled. "Ouch!" He clenched his teeth and dropped to the ground behind the kitchen island.

"Oh, hell!" Derek darted toward him. "What's wrong?"

Russ groaned and panted.

"Answer us!" Bren shouted.

"Like, not again!"

Derek pointed. "Russ, you're a—"

"Woman!" Bren blurted out.

"Like, no way," she screamed, pushing the mass of blonde hair back. "Why is this totally happening to me?" Her voice trembled as tears streamed down her face.

"Hey, I've got you!" Derek grabbed an arm and helped her up.

"Here, take this." Bren pulled off his pajama top and slung it over Russ' shoulders. "No more walking around shirtless for you."

"Majorly not." She leaned forward, snatched up the sweat pants that had fallen to her ankles and yanked them to her waist.

"We need Dr. Munson," Derek stated.

Bren turned. "I'll call Raymond."

"I'm way thirsty..." She sniveled while reaching for the refrigerator door. "I so need something to drink."

"I'll get it for you." Derek held her arm. "What do you want? Water, soda, some milk"

"Like, some gin...and a lot of it!"

Derek smirked. "You don't drink."

She wiped away some stray tears. "With all this hideous stuff happening to me, I might totally make an exception...and add along some pills for good measure."

Bren entered the kitchen. "Well, you can ask Dr. Munson for a prescription. He's on his way here."

"In the meantime, here's a bottle of water." Derek handed it to her.

"Thanks!" She took it. "Like, when did you shave off your goatee?"

"I didn't." Derek grasped his chin. "Where the hell is it?"

Bren pointed. "Your sideburns are gone too."

"Hell, no—"

Bren's mouth dropped wide open.

Derek gripped his stomach, let out an awful moan and fell against the refrigerator.

"It's totally happening," Russ emphasized. She grasped his hand. "You're so becoming a girl—"

"No way, man," Derek yelled.

"Like, yes way, woman," Russ echoed.

Derek pushed by them, held onto his underwear and jeans, high-tailed it to the bathroom and locked out the roommates.

"Let us in," Bren bellowed, banging on door.

"No," came the high-pitched screech.

Russ jiggled the doorknob. "Totally let me in"

"No..." Derek sobbed. "I'm a woman."

"Like, what do you think I am?" Russ uttered.

Bren grinned. "Oh, may I answer that?"

Russ glared. "This is so not the time."

As the door crept opened, there stood a woman with long, wavy red hair and smooth, milky white skin. Heavy tears streamed out of her piercing green eyes and rolled down her pretty, angular face.

"Like, don't cry, honey..." Russ threw her arms around Derek. "I totally grabbed your t-shirt off the couch."

"Thanks!" She wept, taking the t-shirt and putting it on. "I guess I don't need these anymore." A robust kick flung the underwear and jeans out the bathroom door.

"Dr. Munson should be here any moment," Bren stated.

"I hope with a prescription pad." Derek wiped the tears from her eyes.

51

"Why, is it painful?" Bren asked.

"At the beginning it was..." She sniffled. "But now it's just annoying. I liked being a guy much better."

Bren nodded. "Do you know what else is annoying? All these breasts bouncing around and I'm not able to touch any of them. Do you know how long it's been since I've had a girlfriend?"

Russ snickered. "Like, the early 1800's—"

"Or when you dragged a cavewoman by her hair to your prehistoric den!" Derek sneered.

"Well, I can see the solution you both fell into didn't alter your sense of humor," Bren snarled. "You two are still not funny."

"Wait until it happens to you," Derek groused. "We'll see what straws you grasp at."

Bren smirked. "I know what I won't be grasping at."

Bold knocking battered the front door.

"Good, they're here." Bren turned, left the bathroom and answered it.

"Where is Russ?" Raymond entered.

"She's in the bathroom with Derek," Bren replied. "They're both women."

"Both!" Raymond ran into the bathroom. "How are you guys, or shall I say...gals?"

Derek burst into tears and buried her face in Russ' shoulder. "Like, I'm totally fine, but her...not so much."

"Dr. Munson should be here shortly. He had to finish a consultation." Raymond rubbed his forehead. "Do either of you need anything?"

"Would you majorly get her a drink of water?" Russ asked.

Raymond exited the bathroom as Bren entered.

"Go and totally get us a decent shirt to wear," Russ requested. "Like, Dr. Munson will be here any minute, and we still need to be looking our best even though we're enduring the worst."

Bren chuckled. "You should write Hallmark cards."

"Like, move it!" Russ ordered.

"Ok, don't get your panties in a wad," Bren snapped. "Oh, that's right, you don't have any to wear."

Russ swatted at him.

Bren leaped back and left as Raymond walked in with a glass of water. "Here you go."

Russ took it from him and put it to Derek's quivering lips. "Honey, you so need to take a sip of this."

I cannot believe you're both women." Raymond shook his head. "I also cannot call you by your male names, especially in public."

"I've majorly taken care of that matter," Russ uttered.

Bren strolled in. "Here are the shirts you demanded."

Russ snatched them and handed back the empty water glass. "Like, hello!" Her eyebrows creased. "Do you guys totally mind turning your heads?"

Raymond cleared his throat after realizing what was said. "Sorry about that." He and Bren faced the other way at the same time.

Derek and Russ slung the shirts over their shoulders and pulled them down. "Like, we're done."

They both turned back around.

"I'm going to look out the window and watch for the doctor to arrive." Bren walked out of the bathroom.

Raymond looked at his watch. "Mitchell should be arriving soon."

Derek burst into tears again. Russ held tight to her.

"Dr. Munson is here," Bren hollered.

Russ lifted Derek's face. "Like, we need to go out into the living room."

"Ok..." She sniveled. "I feel naked in just a shirt."

Russ stepped back. "The shirt totally covers your junk...or should I say your lack of it, and since we're girls we so have nothing hanging down. I mean, at least the lower half."

"Not comforting," Derek griped, stretching the shirt as far down over her knees as possible.

"Like, are you ready?" Russ asked.

Derek breathed out. "Let's do this."

They left the bathroom, went over to the sofa and sat down.

"Russ, you need to close your legs. I can see your womanly parts," Bren remarked, sitting in an opposite chair. "No more man-spread for you in that condition." His legs were opened wide.

"She crossed them several times before getting it right. "Like, this whole girl thing will totally take some time getting used to."

Derek followed suit then pulled her shirt down over the knees. "Is that good?" she asked.

"Better," Bren replied.

Raymond met Dr. Munson at the door.

"I came as soon as I could." He walked in.

"Thanks," Raymond stated. "I know traffic is a nightmare this time of the day."

"It is a nightmare any time of the day," Dr. Munson added.

Raymond nodded. "How true—"

"Where is my patient?"

"You now have two!" Bren pointed at them. "You'll be pulling double-duty."

"I see that." Dr. Munson walked over to the sofa and held Derek's wrist. "Your pulse is extremely rapid." He opened his medical bag and pulled out his stethoscope. "How are you feeling?"

"Like a woman," she retorted. "This has thrown me all off kilter."

Dr. Munson looked at Russ. "How are you feeling?"

"Like a woman," she responded. "Only I feel totally on kilter."

Bren sneered. "That's because you now have twenty-four hours of breasts to play with."

"You're such a grody pig," Russ quipped.

Bren scowled. "Wow, look who's calling the kettle black?"

"Enough!" Derek belted out. "This is not fun and games."

54

"Everybody calm down," Raymond decreed. "Arguing will get us nowhere."

A hush came over the room.

Dr. Munson looked at Derek. "Would you stand up?"

"Ok." She got off the couch.

Dr. Munson placed his stethoscope on Derek's heart then her lungs. "I need you to breathe deeply. In and out. Again in and out. Now breathe normally." He turned to Russ and repeated the examination. When everything was completed, he issued, "Well, both of your blood pressures, pulses, respiration and temperatures are up a bit. I thought they would be. But I do not feel they are of dire concern."

"So what do we do now?" Derek's eyes again filled with tears.

Dr. Munson grabbed her hand. "In my opinion you both should—"

"Russ has changed back," Bren roared as he hopped up and headed toward the hallway.

"Son, what happened?" Dr. Munson asked.

"I so closed my eyes and thought to myself, 'I want to be Russ. I want to be Russ'...over and over again," he answered, his tone deep and masculine.

Bren ran back into the room and threw him a pair of sweat pants. "Here, put these on."

Derek looked to Russ. "You were so quiet during the change. Usually you're moaning and groaning."

"It totally didn't happen this time." He pulled up the sweat pants. "Like, there was no grody pain."

"Wow, usually it's no pain—no gain," Bren blurted out.

"Really?" Derek threw him a bitter look.

"Russ, again your thoughts brought you back to being a man, and there was no pain this time?" Dr. Munson questioned. "You must be quite relieved."

He nodded. "You're majorly reading my mind—"

"And trust me," Bren chimed in. "That's not an easy task with so little thought process going on."

55

Russ glared at him. "Like, my mind is way cool."

"It's more like frostbitten." Bren stared back.

"Knock it off," Derek screamed. "I'm not doing this today." She jumped up from the sofa and paced with her hands fidgeting. "Why can't I change back?"

"You probably need to be more focused." Dr. Munson put his hands on her shoulders. "Still yourself. Now close your eyes and relax. Concentrate your thoughts on, 'I want to be Derek. I want to be Derek'. Run it through your mind over and over again."

Her forehead scrunched and jaw stiffened as her eyelids sealed shut. Almost a minute had passed when they finally opened. "Nothing happened," she bellowed with balled hands. "It's not working. Why?"

"You need to relax," Dr. Munson replied. "As I watched you, your face was tensing up. Do not tighten it," he stated. "Now close your eyes and shake the tension away."

Derek shut them and shook her whole body.

"Now relax and empty your mind. Clear away all your thoughts..." Dr. Munson stood behind her. "Relax. Now breathe deeply. Now slowly let it out." His tone remained calm and steady. "Inhale. Exhale. Now breathe deeply. Now slowly let it out. Again inhale then exhale. Now think to yourself, 'I want to be Derek. I want to be Derek. I want to be Derek...'" The doctor's voice faded with each syllable until it fell silent."

With the face twitching, she moaned and groaned while clutching her stomach. "Ah...ouch, oh...ouch, ah—"

Dr. Munson stepped aside as Derek turned back into a man.

Gasps were heard.

Bren ran back to the hallway.

"See how easy that was," Dr. Munson declared.

Derek rubbed his chest. "Wow, I'm me!" His manly voice blurted out.

Russ jacked up his thumb. "Like, totally."

Derek grabbed and bear-hugged him.

56

"Dude, you're so going to break me in half."

"Sorry about that, and thanks for calling me, dude."

"Like, whatever," a woman's voice said.

"Russ!" Derek let go. "What're you doing?"

She giggled.

"Did you change on purpose?"

"Totally," came the masculine reply. Russ was back.

"Man, that's so not cool!"

"Way sorry, dude—"

"Derek, here's your jeans." Bren tossed them to him.

"Awesome, thanks!" He put them on. "With all the excitement, I forgot I was naked down below."

"Like, I didn't," came the feminine tone.

"You shouldn't keep changing back and forth..." Bren warned, waggling his finger. "You just might stay that way."

She smiled. "Like, whatever!"

"Could Russ stay that way, Dr. Munson?" Derek asked. "I mean, could any of us get stuck being a woman?"

"I could not say," he answered. "Nothing shows the contrary. Russ has changed sexes a few times and without incident. She seems to be enjoying the new experience."

"But couldn't that be destroying something inside her body, as in brain cells?" Bren questioned. "Russ really doesn't have many to spare."

"As long as my beauty is spared, I totally don't care!"

"I will keep testing you three to see if and how your stats change," Dr. Munson said. "The only issue I feel you might face is your monthly visitor."

"A woman's period." Bren grinned. "Bloating, cramping and irritability will look quite well on her."

"Like, no way," she quipped. "I'll so change back into a guy when that happens."

Dr. Munson shook his head. "That might not suffice—"

"What does that mean? Derek blurted out.

"A woman's menstrual cycle happens every twenty-eight days give or take, and most menstrual periods usually last from 3 to 5 days," he continued. "During menstruation, the lining of the uterus is shed. It flows through the small opening in the cervix and passes out of the body via the vagina."

"That's going to happen to us?" Derek's face contorted.

"If you are between the ages of 10 and 50, it would have to," the doctor reacted. "It is a biological function that needs to transpire if one wants to stay healthy."

"What if Russ was to be a woman for three weeks then turn back into a man, would it null and void those twenty-one days and start over anew when he went back to being female?" Bren asked.

Dr. Munson shrugged. "I have no idea," he answered. "They are normally consecutive days, but with your hormones in such disarray, we will have to wait and see. It could occur in a day, a few weeks, several months or not at all."

"Like, not at all so gets my vote."

Bren smirked. "In a day would go on my ballot."

Russ put her palm up to his face. "I'm way over this conversation."

"That's fine with me..." Bren pushed away her hand. "Consider it over."

"People, can we end this?" Derek grumbled.

Bren nodded. "We're done."

"Like, so done." She tossed her hair to the side.

"Last night, I did some reading on the folklore of that region." Dr. Munson sat on the sofa. "This morning my mother had gone out early so I talked to my aunt. I was told that from the time they were little girls, she and my mother heard stories about some women from the Aztec nation who had become outcasts due to their sexual orientation and other unwelcomed traits. They fled deep into the Amazon jungle and formed their own tribe—"

58

"All women..." Derek grinned. "Where do I sign up for that group?"

Bren snickered. "The only thing you would be signing is your death warrant."

"The doctor continued. "So the story goes, eventually some of the women had sexual relations with the men of a neighboring tribe to keep their meager population from dying out. Supposedly, these men wanted to dominate the women and make them subservient but they broke free and went back to their tribe. With no men to further their existence, they began dying off."

Raymond leaned in. "Do you think the story is true?"

"Well, she is a very old woman who drinks her own hand-made hooch so I am not quite sure." Dr. Munson chuckled. "She and my mother have told me so many tales over the years. Some true; some not so true. The old women in my village enjoy telling colorful stories, and the more colors they add, the better the story." He paused. "However the fable goes, I do not feel I will ever find out the original version."

Bren looked at Russ. "Speaking of an old woman, that's what this one will become if she ends up being stuck as that sex."

"Like, whatever!"

"Did you ask your aunt about some natural formulas we can take?" Derek queried.

Dr. Munson rose up from the sofa. "She has some formulas for organic hormone replacement, but I do not feel it would help with your situation."

"Like, does she have a formula to turn Bren into a frog?"

"Not to my knowledge," the doctor reacted.

Bren smirked. "Well, I guess that means I'll still be a prince."

Russ sneered. "I'd totally say you're more of a pauper."

"Why can't they benefit from hormone therapy?" Raymond questioned.

"Hormones are very powerful," Dr. Munson responded. "As I told you at the hospital, the altering of one's sex involves more than just hormones. This elixir has enlarged organs, gotten into their brain matter, are deep inside hidden cell reservoirs and absorbed into tissue. I am afraid that adding more hormones to the mix could have deadly consequences."

"So we're doomed!" Derek clamored.

"Do not dwell on the negative to bring you down," the doctor suggested. "Think positive thoughts that will uplift."

"I want nothing better than to uplift this woman out of me and leave my boys down where they belong," Bren uttered.

"Should they do anything differently?" Raymond asked.

"Yes, they should come back with me to the hospital where other specialists can monitor them," Dr. Munson retorted. "This is the only way to find out if there is an antidote for their condition."

"How many monitors and other gizmos will we be hooked up to?" Derek enquired.

"Better yet, how many people will be involved in our supposed care?" Bren requested. "Would we be quarantined?"

"To a degree, you gentlemen will most likely experience all three," the doctor claimed. "It would be for your betterment, not to your detriment."

"It would also make the hospital look good having three freaks on their roster," Bren stated. "Just count me out!"

Derek smirked. "Yeah, me too."

"Like, me three."

Dr. Munson exhaled. "The only thing we should do now is let nature take its course," he advised. "Unfortunately, we are in uncharted waters. I referenced several medical journals and there was nothing to speak of. I also looked all this up on the Internet. There were numerous videos of men digitally transforming into women, and on gender-reassignment surgery, but nothing about an actual metamorphosis from male into a female as in your case. Even if I had seen or read something on there, how trustworthy would it be, and what about its validity? Many people have died trying these 'homemade remedies' from unprofessional and unscrupulous individuals presenting themselves as medical personnel."

Heads nodded in agreement.

60

"Thanks, Mitch," Raymond expressed. "I really appreciate you taking time out of your busy schedule to help my boys, and I'm using that term loosely."

The doctor bared a partial smile.

Are we still on for dinner tomorrow?" Raymond asked.

"Most certainly," Dr. Munson answered while picking up his medical bag.

"I'll walk you out," Raymond said.

The doctor smiled. "Goodbye, gentlemen and lady."

"Like, my name is Rue."

Dr. Munson dipped his head as Raymond looked twice at her. They left the apartment.

"Mitch is such a sexy name." Rue purred.

"Down girl!" Bren barked. "You're just like your male counterpart."

"Hey, we need to come up with a strategy," Derek stated. "Then we need to eat and get ready to go to the Back Alley Bar for our stakeout."

"Yes, Logan Price and Henry Prescott will be there," Bren added. "They're supposed to hire that woman tonight."

"I'm so not hungry," Rue uttered. "I majorly want to take a shower."

Bren snickered. "Ladies are usually first."

"Like, beauty before the beast." Rue giggled.

"Aren't you changing back into a man?" Derek asked.

"And why would I totally do that?" She whipped her hair around. "I'm so taking a long, hot, steamy shower and experiencing what it feels like to be a woman." She went to the bathroom, closed the door and locked it.

Derek smirked. "You know what she's going to do in the shower, right?"

"What?"

"The same thing he does in there as a man."

Bren raised an eyebrow. "Oh, you're not suggesting—"

61

"Let's just say you're cleaning the shower."

"Gross!" Bren blurted out. "Not even close."

Derek cracked up.

"Why doesn't she do that in bed like everybody else?"

Derek shook his head. "Because Russ or whatever her current name is, isn't like everybody else."

"Yuck!" Bren grimaced. "This is going to be a very long night."

Chapter 5

A broken neon sign flickered in the front window of the Back Alley Bar as the detectives drove into the gravel-laden parking lot. With dust-filled air swirling about, Bren parked next to a sturdy garbage bin and shut off the engine.

"Thank the sweet Lord for our GPS system!" He removed the keys. "Now instead of being an hour late, we're only thirty minutes."

"It didn't help that Russ—"

"Like, my name is Rue."

"Sorry," Derek rendered. "We would've been here sooner if you had come as Russ."

"I'm so being blamed for this?" Rue pulled down the visor and looked into the mirror. "It was Bren's hideous driving that made us way late." She slathered on some lipstick.

"You have your nerve..." Bren scoffed. "I aced my driving test, and I'm certainly the better driver of us three."

"I meant that if you would've totally stopped where I wanted to shop in the first place, we would've been here way earlier." Rue fluffed up her hair. "Like, I almost broke out in hives in that first store."

"What are you whining about?" Bren scowled. "It was Saks Fifth Avenue."

Rue pursed her lips. "It's so where old, rich ladies go to die."

"Watch it..." Bren snarled. "My mother shops there."

"Like, whatever!" She sprayed hairspray on her tussled tresses. "You always think your way is the best."

63

"Because, usually it is." Bren waved his hands about frantically. "Stop with that stuff," he shouted. "What're you trying to do, put me in an early grave?"

"If only," Rue reacted.

"Ouch!" Derek belted out.

"Don't put this on me." Bren pointed at her. "It's because you came as a woman—"

"Instead of coming as a guy and wearing something you already have at home like jeans, a T-shirt and your Converse high-tops..." Derek leaned forward. "You had to come as a girl, and we had to stop for you to shop for something to wear tonight."

Bren look in her direction. "That wouldn't have been so bad, but then you went berserk because there was a sale and bought half the store."

"Not just a sale, but a clearance sale," Rue uttered. "Like, that's on a whole other level. I think one can be so arrested for the criminal offense of walking by a clearance rack without looking. It's way considered accessory after the fact or something like that, and I don't need some grody ticket or a jail sentence by the fashion police."

"What?" Derek scrunched his face.

"Let me handle this..." Bren interceded. "If there was a crime for taking forever to look at garments on sale, you would get the death penalty."

"And you're feeding into her, why?" Derek asked.

"I totally saved some major loot buying things I needed on sale." Rue powdered her nose.

"Oh, you needed that outfit you're wearing?" Bren queried. "It reveals more flesh than a Band-Aid. Most of your legs are showing and the shirt—and I'm using that term loosely, exposes three-quarters of your breasts. I mean, they're mostly hanging out, not to mention you purchased five more like it. Then you bought the six pairs of high heels or should I say stilts to balance on, and also four purses that barely holds a cell phone with car keys—"

64

"Bras, underwear, jewelry and let's not forget the wad of makeup." Derek interjected. "You've also got hair products up the wazoo—"

"And you don't even own a blow dryer," Bren stated. "What's up with that?"

"Like, I'm so getting myself one," Rue replied. "A woman needs to be majorly prepared for every situation."

"What situation requires a bagful of make-up?" Derek asked.

"For when you two so turn into chicks...or should I say broads," Rue answered.

"That's not going to happen to me," Bren declared. "I'm teeming with testosterone."

Derek puffed. "Hell, I'm brimming to the rim too."

"I wasn't running on empty when I totally changed." Rue misted on some perfume.

"Speaking of the change, why didn't you come as a guy?" Bren posed.

"I'm totally doing this because it looks way better for a girl and guy to enter a bar together, like they're on some kind of date, as in you and I," Rue retorted. "We'll so go inside like lovebirds and sit down close to where the meeting is being held." Her face beamed. "Derek, you can come in inconspicuously and sit on the other side of their conversation. That way we can hear all sides without them being suspicious."

"I can't believe you thought of that plan all by yourself," Bren remarked.

She swooshed her hand. "Like, if a couple totally goes into a bar, nobody really bats a lash...but if three good-looking guys go into a seedy joint together, it could totally make a drunk hick uneasy, especially if his woman is with him."

"She's quite right," Derek admitted. "This is a neighborhood bar with regulars and if we go in as three guys, we'll get the evil eye. But if I go in by myself and sit on one side of the bar, and you both go in together and act like you're out on a date, you could sit right next to me and nobody's the wiser."

"Again, I can't believe you thought of that plan all by yourself," Bren remarked.

65

Rue tilted her head. "What do you totally think I am—a space cadet?"

"I think he was leaning more toward an airhead," Derek replied.

"Well, you do have three strikes against you," Bren declared. "You're a blonde woman from California."

Rue huffed. "Like, you so need to take that back."

"Why?" Bren asked. "I was giving you a compliment, more or less."

"Derek, will you be my date instead of this chauvinist pig?"

"Hell no, I'm not getting between you two lovebirds."

Rue leaned over, snatched the keys out of the ignition and got out of the car. She trotted to the back of the car, popped the trunk and took out a purse. After opening it, her Olympus S-711 microcassette recorder with voice activation was pulled out. *Like, this is totally cool. I can so eavesdrop on the suspects during their conversation without them even knowing.*

"Man, you ought to apologize to her," Derek urged.

"Then you come with me," Bren pleaded. "I need some support."

"You need some testosterone."

Bren smirked as both men got out and headed toward the back of the car.

"I was just playing with you," Bren noted.

Rue ignored him and continued digging around in the truck.

Bren grabbed her arm. "I'm sorry!"

She faced him with pouted lips.

"It's just I'm a little peeved I didn't think of your plan first," he continued. Bren looked at the ground and kicked some gravel. "You know I'm the smart one and all."

"Is that your major idea of an apology?" Her gaze was firm.

"Why, do you accept it?" Bren asked.

Rue jacked her head back. "Like, should I?"

66

"I think so," he replied. "It did come from my heart after all."

She snickered. "That totally dark and cold place?"

"Yes." Bren kept his head down.

Rue exhaled. "Like, I guess so, but on one condition—"

"What?"

"You need to help me pick out some fierce heels to go with my sexy and stunning ensemble."

"Any pair, as long as they are black," Bren issued.

Derek leaned against the car. "And you know this, how?"

"Not that it's any of your business, but when I was a little boy, I would sit at my mother's makeup mirror and watch her..." Bren reminisced. "I remember this one night she was getting ready for a dinner party and asked my father to grab her shoes out of the closet. He came back with a pair and she chastised him saying, 'Those shoes are blue and I am wearing lilac. Please, hand me my black ones. Black goes with everything.' She was so elegant."

"Like, he's right!" Rue agreed. "Just totally read that in one of the fashion magazines I bought."

"Well, throw them on," Derek commented. "I'm ready for a beer."

"I'll so wear the black heels with the zippers on the side." She pulled them out.

"Just hurry up," Derek urged. "I'm thirsty."

Rue flinched. "Like, there's no fast in the word—fashion."

"Oh, man," Derek quipped. "Where's my buddy, Russ?"

"Russ is way asleep, but Rue is totally awake."

Bren yawned. "May we go?"

"Wait!" Rue beckoned. "Like, how does my makeup look?"

"Lord, give me strength," Bren muttered.

Derek leaned in. "Um...it looks, ah...good."

"Blanche totally did it for me." Rue smiled "Raymond totally told her about our predicament, so when I walked in, she couldn't believe

67

her eyes. She put her knitting down and stared at me. I was majorly weirded out until she finally told me I was gorgeous."

"I bet she did!" Derek popped off. "With her being old-fashioned and whatnot, I'm really surprised you wore any of her clothes."

"Like, I only wore her grody dress until I could majorly hit a store on the way here." Rue opened her compact to look at her face. "She totally taught me how to paint the face and blend my eye colors."

"Are you sure it wasn't Crayola who put it on?" Bren sneered.

Rue balked. "It was so called Cover Girl."

"Well, I call it heavy." Bren slammed the trunk.

"Well, I call it totally hot." Rue smirked.

"I'd say hot to trot," Bren added. "I thought you looked better without all that war-paint covering your face. Not to mention Blanche's dress refined your appearance."

"That was so beat at the seams." She looked at Derek for security.

"I think you look really awesome."

"Down boy...now sit," Bren commanded. "I don't want you two mating."

Derek huffed. "He's my...she's my friend, you idiot. I know she's still Russ."

"Do you?" Bren asked.

Derek turned his head. "Let's go."

Rue pushed by Bren. "Like, you need to be totally supportive!"

"By the look of things, so does the bra you're not wearing, but who's counting?"

"I'm counting, and when I hit ten, you'd better be at the door of this hole," Derek demanded. "And here's a heads up. A mouthy college guy doesn't do well in this kind of atmosphere, so jack it back."

"Like, this place is such a total dive," Rue stated.

"I bet it's one of those hoodlum bars," Derek remarked. "The kind where regulars pick a fight with the new guy, beat him to death with pool sticks then toss his body into a dumpster."

Bren scoffed. "If this place is good enough for governmental bigwigs then it's good enough for us."

They arrived at the door.

"Listen, I'll go in first, then you two come in and get noticed," Derek insisted. "It'll take the heat off of me."

"Don't worry, honey..." Rue shimmied her body. "I'll totally get noticed."

"Cool!" Derek rubbed his hands together. "This is my kind of stakeout."

"Remember, we're not here to party," Bren declared. "We've a job to do and we don't want to blow our cover."

"You know I don't drink alcohol," Rue uttered. "Like, it makes me too woozy."

"We all know," Bren stated. "I was talking to Derek."

"Duh, you don't think I know that? Besides, I only drink beer. It's you that enjoys the liquor."

"Has somebody forgotten the McGillicuddy case a few months back?" Bren related. "I remember someone getting quite drunk and sleeping with our client's wife."

"She seduced me with liquor," Derek reacted. "I still think she slipped me something."

"Oh, something was definitely slipped." Bren jeered.

"I'm done with this conversation," Derek claimed. "I'll just stick with beer from now on."

"Like, let's go inside." Rue nestled up to Bren. "I so want to show off my luscious appearance."

He grinned. "I see you're taking this role seriously."

"I totally have to." She shook her head. "You so won't pull it off."

"Speaking of pulling it..." Derek yanked the door handle.

"Just get inside," Bren grumbled.

69

Derek entered the bar and passed by a beautiful woman. Logan Price and Henry Prescott were hunched together having a secretive pow-wow. He continued to the corner of the bar, pulled up a stool and sat down.

"I'll be right with you, pal," the bartender roared.

Derek nodded.

Bren and Rue entered next. She wiggled and jiggled up to the bar and sat down on a stool next to the beautiful woman. The bartender left off with a customer and walked up to her.

"Well, hello there, pretty lady..." His voice was rough and husky. "What's your pleasure?"

Rue smiled. "Like, I'll take a Diet Pepsi, please." She batted her lashes.

"Don't overdo it," Bren whispered. He stood close to her.

"What can I get you, sir?" the bartender asked.

"I'll have a Tanqueray and tonic with a wedge of lime, please."

"Coming right up," the bartender stated. He walked toward Derek. "What're you having, buddy?"

"I'll take a Bud Light."

The bartender made their drinks and after serving Derek, moseyed down and stationed himself across from Rue.

"I love your shoes," the beautiful woman said. "Are they Prada?"

"I totally don't know?" Rue smiled at her. "Like, I'm just becoming a fashion plate."

"You look like the entire dish." She crossed her legs. "My name is Lydia Reome."

"Like, my name is Rue Munroe, and thank you for that delicious compliment."

"You are welcome," Lydia said. "It is nice to meet you."

Rue leaned in. "I so love your accent. Like, where are you from?"

"I am from France," Lydia replied. "Where are you from with your style of speech?"

"I'm totally a California girl," Rue answered.

"I heard it was a beautiful state," Lydia mentioned. "Full of movie stars and sunshine."

"Like, the same is said for your country." Rue angled her head. "So, what brought you here from France? A boyfriend?" She stared into Lydia's eyes. "Maybe you're a career girl with a majorly fabulous job."

"I wish it was so glamorous."

Rue reached into her purse and turned on the micro recorder.

"I am a physicist," Lydia stated.

"Wow, you're a triple threat!" Rue boasted. "Like, you've got brains, beauty and a major body—"

"Plus, I make my own money."

Rue leaned in and whispered. "I totally feel that's what men are for."

Lydia raised her drink. "Here is to men."

Rue clanked her glass against it. "Like, especially the wealthy and powerful ones."

They both shook with laughter.

"Thank you," Lydia said. "I needed that release. I am a mass of nerves. The gentleman on the end has summoned me here to conduct an interview for a position at his company. I want to make a good first impression, but the two of them have been huddled together this whole time with their own private discussion."

"Like, let them huddle." Her hand swished to and fro. "We'll totally have our own private girl talk."

"We call it gossip in my country."

"Like, we do too." Rue giggled. "Girl code is totally international."

"Yes, it is." Lydia laughed.

Like, she has no clue that I'm a detective working her for information. "So, who is the man on the far end?"

"His name is Henry Prescott," Lydia replied. "He owns a chemical company and wants to employ me to perfect some special formula. The one next to me is Logan Price. He is the Speaker of the House..." She leaned in and whispered. "The White House."

71

"That's why he totally looks familiar," Rue remarked. "I've so seen him on television with our President."

"I am dating him."

"Like, he must be a powerful man."

Lydia snickered. "Yes, and one that is wrapped around my little finger."

"You go, girl!" Rue put a hand to her chest. "That's majorly awesome."

Logan turned toward Lydia. "Henry's ready to talk with you. He'll switch seats with me."

Lydia looked to Rue. "Please, do not leave without saying goodbye. I do not have any girlfriends here in the States."

"Like, one can never have too many girlfriends."

Lydia nodded. "It should take me but a moment." She turned around and faced Henry.

Rue got up and leaned into Bren. "My micro recorder is totally catching their every word."

"Great." He put his arm around her. "I have to hand it to you. Even though you're a dingbat sometimes, you come through when it's crunch time."

"Like, are you getting sloshed?" Rue asked. "I would so swear you just gave me a compliment."

"So it seems," Bren replied. "You know as Russ you irritate me, but as Rue...you're actually tolerable."

"It totally must be the alcohol talking."

"This is my first drink."

"I'm so cutting you off if you continue with the praise." Rue sat down and crossed her legs. She leaned back to hear the conversation. It was quieted, but still audible. She knew her micro recorder could pick up any discussion up to twenty feet away with clarity. There wasn't a worry.

"With that being said, I'd like to extend the position of lead physicist at Prescott Chemicals to you," Henry was saying. "You'll be working with my lead chemist on a classified formula. It'll be

72

your top priority with the understanding you are to tell nobody about this."

"I will say nothing, sir." Her head shook. "You have my word."

"Good!" Henry gulped down his drink. "Logan's driver can bring you tomorrow, let's say around 1:00pm, to sign the necessary paperwork. We can discuss your salary and other tidbits then."

"Yes, that will be fine." Lydia agreed.

"I want you to start Friday morning at 8:30am." Henry specified. "Depending on the formula's outcome, you might have to work this weekend. Will there be an issue?"

Without hesitation, she reacted, "I will be there on time and ready to work."

"Well, I guess that concludes our meeting." Henry stood up. "It's time for me to get my coat and head out of this joint, but first I'm going to find out if Slim Sleazen needs a ride home. I heard the old drunken buzzard staggered into the road last week and was clipped by car."

"Don't you pay his tab every month?" Logan asked.

"Yeah, that ugly mug hasn't two pennies to rub together, but he rubbed my old man the wrong way so he's aces in my book." After nodding his head, Henry walked away.

Logan grinned, hopped off the bar stool and gave Lydia a big hug. "Just think..." His voice lowered. "Our formula will finally be perfected."

"Yes, and I will have a brand new perfume sample."

"Just make sure you're extremely careful not to be seen."

"I will," Lydia whispered. "You do not need to worry."

"With this crew I've employed, worry is my middle name." His head tilted. "Now you look worried."

"I thought they pulled out of Prescott Chemicals and are working at an old farmhouse—"

"They were...until Henry saw how much it'd cost to revamp the old distillery," Logan related. "Now they're just bringing back a minimal amount to perfect."

73

"What if the police were to come again?"

"It's the FBI's case now, and with my sources in the Bureau, I'll hail an alert that they're coming—"

"I'm leaving," Henry declared, strolling up. "Lydia, I'll see you tomorrow at 1:00pm." He looked aside. "Logan, are you staying?"

"We're heading out in a moment," he replied. "I still have to stop by the White House tonight and take care of some paperwork for the President." His face beamed. "I like that word—President."

"Especially if it's in front of your name," Henry remarked.

"President Price..." Logan crowed with his chin up. "It does have a nice ring to it."

"President Prescott doesn't sound half-bad either." Henry chuckled.

"Vice-President Prescott is better suited for you." Logan grinned.

"V.P. Prescott does flow nicely off the tongue. Well, goodnight all." Henry turned and exited.

"That went well," Logan claimed. "I'll get our coats."

"Wait!" Lydia stopped him. "Since you have to work tonight, I will stay and associate with my new girlfriend."

"Are you sure?" Logan questioned. "How will you get back to my place?"

"I will call a taxi and go back to the Alabaster Hotel," Lydia answered. "Besides, all my toiletries, shoes and wardrobe are there. Not to mention the perfume bottle to collect the formula per our deal."

"You need to be careful—"

"I am a woman," she interjected. "We know how to be cautious."

Logan breathed out. "May I meet your friend?"

"Yes." Lydia turned and tapped Rue on the shoulder. "I want to introduce you to my boyfriend."

"Sure, totally."

"Rue Munroe, this gentleman here is Logan Price."

74

He took her hand.

"Like, it's a major honor meeting the Speaker of the House!" Rue gushed.

"Please, it's an honor meeting such a beautiful woman." Logan dipped his head. "I'm glad that Lydia has met a new friend."

Rue smiled. "She's totally a wonderful woman."

"That, I know." Logan kissed Lydia on the cheek.

"I will see you tomorrow after my meeting with Mr. Prescott," she said. "Goodnight."

"Goodnight." Logan stepped back. "Nice meeting you, Miss Munroe."

"Like, the pleasure was all mine." Rue watched him exit then turned her head. "So, how was your interview?"

"I garnered the position," Lydia responded.

Rue gently clapped her hands. "Super-duper! Let me totally buy you a congratulatory cocktail." She motioned to the bartender.

"Only one salutary drink," Lydia stated. "I need to look fresh tomorrow."

The bartender approached. "What can I get you beautiful ladies?"

"I'll so have another Diet Pepsi and a cocktail for my friend, please." Rue requested.

Lydia smiled. "I will have a Chivas Regal on the rocks, please."

The bartender grinned then strayed away.

"Ooh, you like the hard stuff," Rue quipped.

"Yes. In France, a person is bottle-fed it from an infant."

"Like, are you serious?"

Lydia laughed. "I might have exaggerated a wee bit, but we do start young."

The bartender arrived with drinks in hand. "These are on the guy at the end of the bar."

Both women looked over at Derek as he lifted his bottle of beer in acknowledgement.

"My boyfriend may have a great position, but I wish he looked like him," Lydia remarked.

"He is totally cute." Rue giggled. "Like, maybe we should personally go up and thank him."

"No!" Lydia shook her head. "A lady never approaches a gentleman."

"There are no ladies here," Rue blurted out. "We're women, and we majorly go after what we want."

Lydia winked. "I just adore your American customs!"

They arose off their stools and walked up to Derek.

"Like, thank you for the drinks," Rue uttered.

Lydia twisted a lock of hair around her finger. "Yes, thank you."

He nodded. "My name is Derek."

"Mine is Rue, and my friend's name is Lydia."

"Cool!" Derek grinned at them.

"Like, no way!" Rue stepped back. "I totally forgot about my boyfriend." She spun on her heels and zipped away.

Derek and Lydia watched as she wiggled back with Bren in tow.

Rue smiled. "This is my majorly yummy boyfriend."

A hand jutted out. "The name's Derek."

"I'm Bren." He clasped and shook it.

"This is Lydia..." Derek gestured toward her. "And I'm pretty sure you know your girlfriend's name."

Laughter broke out.

"Now that we have the introductions out of the way, would anybody care for another drink?" Bren asked.

"I'll take a Bud Light," Derek replied.

"May I have a Chivas Regal on the rocks?" Lydia asked.

"Of course, beautiful," Bren answered.

"Sweetie!" Rue glared at him.

Bren cleared his throat. "What may I get you—honey?"

"I'll totally take another Diet Pepsi—dear."

Bren turned to hail the bartender, lost his footing and fell to his knees. Derek jumped off the bar stool as Rue bent down to help pick him up. Lydia stood as they brought him to his feet.

"Are you ok, my man?" Derek asked.

"Like, what totally happened?" Rue clung to his arm.

"I became very dizzy," Bren replied.

Derek pulled up a bar stool with his free hand. "Here, sit."

Bren eased onto it. "I'm sorry. I feel like such a fool."

"No, please, do not," Lydia spoke up.

"She's so right," Rue uttered. "Like, there are no fools here."

Bren rubbed his head. "I should go home."

"Totally," Rue declared.

Bren kept his head down.

"I'll help you get him to the car," Derek mentioned.

Rue turned to Lydia. "I'm so sorry about this," she stated. "Like, he's obviously not feeling well."

"Take your man home," Lydia insisted. "I will write down my telephone number and you call me tomorrow."

"That would be totally awesome." Rue smiled. She grabbed one of Bren's arms as Derek grabbed the other. They lifted him up off the barstool.

Lydia pulled a pen out of her purse and wrote down the number on a napkin from the bar. "Here, put this someplace safe. I am at the Alabaster Hotel, room 604...and for goodness sakes, do not worry about me. I will take a taxi home."

Rue snatched the napkin and stuffed it down her cleavage. "Derek, would you make sure Lydia gets home, please?"

"Don't worry," he replied. "I've got it covered. We'll split a taxi."

The two of them helped Bren out of the bar as Lydia looked on. They brought him to the car and leaned him against it.

"Bren, what's up?" Derek asked.

"I don't know," he answered. "I feel so weird. I shouldn't have had that second Tanqueray and tonic."

Derek held onto him. "You've drank three times that before and never got sick."

Rue rummaged through his pants pocket and pulled out a set of keys. She unlocked the door.

"Something's wrong," Bren mumbled, raising his hand to his head. "I feel..." His eyes rolled back as he fell to the side.

"Rue, help me!" Derek yelled.

"Like, oh my God, what's wrong?" she screamed.

"I don't know," Derek retorted. "He just dropped."

"Let's totally get him into the car!"

They dragged his limp body onto the backseat.

"Bren!" Derek slapped his face. "Wake up!" He slapped it again.

"Is he breathing?" Rue squawked.

Bren groaned.

"Hurry, you need to take him home."

She nodded and hopped into the driver's seat. Derek slammed the backseat door and ran to her window.

"Like, please be careful," Rue uttered. "It's totally got to be the alcohol affecting something in his brain."

"I'm only drinking beer," Derek countered. "I hardly ever touch the hard stuff."

Rue grabbed his hand. "Like, please..." Her eyes welled up.

"Ok, ok!" Derek threw up his hands. "I won't have anymore."

Rue dashed the tears on her face. "Like, totally pump Lydia for info and make sure she gets to the Alabaster Hotel—safe and sound."

"I've got this covered." Derek stuck out his finger. "Now go!"

"Like, bye!" Rue peeled away. She opened the glove compartment, grabbed her cell phone and frantically dialed a number.

"Hello—"

"Raymond!" Rue bawled. "Bren is way sick and has totally passed out, and I don't know how to get home from here since he'd never let me drive."

"Calm down and listen to me." Raymond instructed. "The GPS system has a reverse coordinate on it."

"Like, it does?" She sniffled.

"Yes," Raymond replied. "It's the second button on the left."

"Ok." She reached for it. "Like, what do I do?"

"Tap it twice and the longitude and latitude should about-face."

"Way!" Rue squealed. "It so switched."

"Great," Raymond stated. "Now just let it do its job and come home."

"I'm so there."

"Ouch, ah...ouch," Bren howled. "Ouch, oh...my stomach, ah—"

"What's that noise?" Raymond asked. "What's wrong?"

"Bren is totally moaning and groaning and—"

"Oh, my stomach...ouch, it's killing me. Ouch, it hurts so much! Ah...the cramps, oh...they really, oh...ouch, ah—"

"Maybe, you should bring him to the emergency room," Raymond suggested.

"I so know what's going on!" Rue turned around to look at Bren. Suddenly, a horn blew. She looked up and almost side-swiped an oncoming car.

"Like, oh my God," she screeched, spinning the steering wheel. The car jerked out of the opposing lane, just missing another car.

"What just happened?"

"Raymond, I almost got us into a major accident."

"Ouch, ah...ouch, oh—"

"Why, what's going on?" Raymond questioned.

"Like, Bren is so—"

"I'm so, what?" Bren puffed and panted.

79

"Totally brace yourself—"

"Why?" he grunted.

Rue felt the thrashing and bashing against the back of her seat. As the moans and groans amplified, a loafer flew by her head and landed on the dashboard.

"Like, you're so turning into—"

"Turning into what?" came the feminine outburst.

"A woman." Rue exhaled. "Hello, Brie."

"Brie!" Her high-pitched shriek was deafening.

"Who is Brie?" Raymond asked.

"Like, what's left of Bren," Rue responded.

Sobbing dampened the air. "Raymond, I am who she said I am."

"Rue, what the devil is going on?"

"Raymond, totally meet Brie, the newest addition to the family."

"What am I going to do?" The weeping continued.

Rue looked in the rearview mirror. "Stop whining like a man and totally deal with it as a woman."

"Never!" Brie sneered. "I know, I'll think hard that I'm a man." Everything went quiet for a moment. "It's not working! Why isn't it working?"

"Alcohol could way be our Achilles' heel," Rue replied.

"If it is, we need to warn Derek," Brie clamored.

"Where is he?" Raymond asked.

"Like, Derek is with Lydia, the one we we're tailing," Rue retorted.

Raymond gasped. "Oh, no!"

"Oh, yes!" Rue huffed. "And we can't warn him because his cell phone is totally in the glove compartment."

"That's right," Brie added. "We didn't want to lose them and have our identities revealed."

"You need to go back to get him," Raymond decreed.

Rue clutched the steering wheel. "Like, I'll turn the car around and get her."

"You mean—him," Raymond countered.

"By the time we totally get to the Back Alley Bar, he'll no longer be Derek," Rue uttered. "She'll be so known as Darla."

"Who?" Brie asked.

"Re-coordinate the GPS system," Raymond directed. "Go get our detective."

Rue flung her hair to the side. "Like, latitude and longitude—here we come!"

Chapter 6

Derek opened his heavy eyes and slowly scanned across the ceiling. He realized it wasn't familiar and lifted his head off the pillow.

Oh, man, do I feel like hell.

He pushed some hair away from his face and looked around.

This isn't my room. A panic jilted him.

Where am I?

Derek turned his head to the right.

That's definitely not my chair.

He moved his head to the left.

And who's this next to me?

Derek centered his head on the pillow, closed his eyes and grasped at the disheveled images jarring his mind.

Ok, let me see. The last place I remember...um, is that bar...yeah, the Back Alley Bar...and now I'm here. Where is here?

He sat up. The blankets fell from his neck onto his lap and after yanking them past his knees, Derek was mortified to see the body of a woman.

Oh, hell no!

She grabbed her breasts which further sealed the fate.

When did this happen?

Derek looked for an exit strategy then leaned over to identify the bed partner.

Damn, it's Lydia Reome!

Derek gently got out of the bed, so as not to wake her sleeping companion.

I need to change back into a man before Lydia wakes up and catches me.

She closed her eyes.

I'm a man...I'm a man...I'm a man!

Derek opened her eyes and looked.

Damn it! It didn't work. I'll have to do it again.

She shut her eyes.

I want to be Derek...I want to be Derek...I want to be Derek!

She opened them and peered down.

Aw, man...still nothing. I'm stuck being a woman. I need to get out of here before Lydia discovers me, and this damn secret.

Derek noticed her clothes on a nearby chair. She crept to them and put on the jeans, but they slid down her legs to the floor.

I need to tighten them.

Derek pulled the jeans back up, slid the belt on the last hole and buckled it. Again they fell to the floor. Panicked, she snuck up to Lydia's closet, opened it and grabbed the first hanger.

This brown dress should do. I'm hoping she won't miss it.

Derek bent down to look for shoes.

These brown ones will have to do. They've got to match. That's what Rue would say, and I'm in no mood to hear her recite the rules of fashion etiquette.

She exhaled.

Why am I thinking of Rue in a time like this? I should be concentrating on getting the hell out of here.

Derek tip-tocd into the bathroom, quietly closed the door and switched on the light. She turned, looked into the mirror and balked.

Oh, hell no! I look nasty...and my hair is a matted mess. Where did all these waves come from?

83

Derek grabbed the brush from the counter and whipped it through the red mass. She splashed some cold water on her face and dried it off.

That will have to do.

Once dressed, she crammed her feet into the shoes, shut off the light and gradually opened the bathroom door. Lydia was fast asleep. Derek went over to the chair and grabbed her clothes. She looked once again at Lydia.

Awesome...still sleeping.

She picked up a pair of sneakers, headed toward the hotel door and walked out.

Whew! I got away with that.

Derek hurried down the hall and got on the elevator. She took it to the lobby and went to the front desk.

"Hello, can I help you?" the clerk asked.

"Yes, I need to use your phone," Derek replied. "I've seemed to have misplaced my purse, and I need to call my friend to pick me up."

The clerk grinned and put the phone on the counter. "Here you go."

"Thank you." She smiled, grabbed the receiver and pressed the various digits.

"Like, hello?"

"Russ?"

"It's Rue...and who is this?"

"It's Derek."

"You're totally a girl."

"You think?"

"Like, it's about time you called!" Rue scolded. "Someone's been a little naughty, haven't they?"

Derek's panic level rose. "Not now! I need to be picked up."

"From where?"

84

"I'm at Lydia's hotel," Derek replied. "Do you know where it is?"

"The Alabaster on Huntington Street, right?"

"Yes, come pick me up," Derek pleaded. "I'm in the lobby."

"Are you totally wearing your clothes from last night?"

"No, I snatched a brown dress and some brown shoes from Lydia's closet."

"Yuck, did you just say brown?"

"Yeah, so what?" Derek snarled.

"Like, you couldn't have found something in pink?"

"I have a wicked hangover and look like hell, so the last thing I'm caring about right now is my wardrobe," she uttered through gritted teeth.

"I totally get it, but a little black dress would've made you look so stylish."

Derek smiled at the clerk then looked away with her jaw clenched. "Not compared to the big black eye you're going to be styling when I get a hold of you."

"Ooh, an unstylish and aggressive chick," Rue quipped. "I'm not so sure I want to be seen with such a dowdy girl." She paused. "On the other hand, an ugly girl would totally make me look way more beautiful—"

"Are you serious?" Derek squawked. "Just hurry up!"

"Like, you need to simmer way down," Rue demanded. "A woman should never raise her voice in public. It's so not becoming. I majorly read that in one of my glamour magazines."

"There are people everywhere and I look like hell, so please, no more about my lack of fashion sense or my unglamorous foghorn. Just get here now. Bye!" Derek hung up the phone and glanced at the clerk. "Thank you, again. You're a lifesaver."

"Nothing doing," he said. "Enjoy your day."

Derek smiled, turned and walked to the front of the hotel. After putting on her coat, she left and went outside to lean against a tree.

Just keep your head down.

85

Several minutes later, Rue came whizzing around the corner and stopped. Derek yanked open the door, jumped in and slammed it shut.

"What's up with totally wearing a man's jacket over that way hideous outfit?" Rue asked. "You could've at least grabbed a fierce coat!"

Derek glared at her. "I've got a splitting headache and need to go home, so shut your face and drive this car before my temper explodes all over you."

"Like, whatever!" Rue shifted into drive and pulled away. After a couple of blocks, she tossed her hair to the side. "Can I totally say just one thing?"

Derek inhaled. "Just one."

"I so left some of my fashion magazines on your bed to read," Rue noted. "You'd majorly benefit from the articles which seem to be written with you in mind."

Derek exhaled as she rolled her eyes.

"Those shoes need to be totally incinerated along with that heinous dress." Rue uttered, swiping her finger from the bottom up. "Even charred polyester is a way better color choice than that mess you've thrown together."

Derek glared. "Well, Christie Brinkley, we all can't be natural-born fashionistas like you, especially when I'm rushing out of a hotel room as a first-time woman grabbing clothes on the fly."

"Like, that's no excuse!" Rue ribbed. "Some people go to jail for their first offense, but with that outfit, you'd get 20 to life, Darla."

"Who's going to arrest me, the Kardashian girls?" She sneered. "And what's with the Darla crap?"

"You totally need to use a girl's name in this condition, so that's what I've named you."

"Don't even try it."

"Like, I can't call you Derek if you're undercover as a woman."

"That will never happen."

"We've been given such an awesome gift to enhance our detective work," Rue remarked. "The ability to change sexes—our identities in the blink of an eye is majorly cool, so remember that."

Darla was quiet for a moment then pointed her finger. "Just remember, when I'm in this condition I'll let you get away with it. But when I'm Derek, don't try it!"

"Like, I can so handle that." Rue dug around in her purse. She took out a lipstick, looked into the rearview mirror and applied some.

Darla grabbed the steering wheel. "Ah, can you please watch the road, and not worry about how you look?"

"A girl should always look her best," Rue handed it over. "You should totally consider using some."

Darla put up the palm of her hand. "I don't think so."

"Like, it's so your loss." Rue slid it back into her purse.

"Maybe it's my gain," Darla countered. "You've got to realize that I'm different from you. Just because you wear lipstick doesn't mean I'm going to wear it."

"It would totally make you look way prettier."

"My head is throbbing so can we change the subject?"

"Like, whatever!

"Thank you."

"Did you totally get information from Lydia?"

"If I did, I don't remember."

"Like, what went on last night?"

Darla leaned her head against the window. "I haven't the foggiest clue."

"I so can't wait until I get Lydia's version of the events."

"Me too." Darla closed her eyes.

"I've got some way juicy gossip for you."

"Enlighten me."

"Like, guess who changed into a major woman last night during a drunken stupor and so cannot change back?"

87

Darla gasped. "Bren."

"I so call her, Brie."

"Are you serious?" Darla clamored. "I bet she's a real humdinger."

"More like a real prissy witch."

"Oh, I'm sure."

"Like, as a boy, I can so deal...but as a girl, she's way intolerable."

"That's just peachy."

"Totally more like the pits."

As they stopped at a red light, a carload of guys motioned for Rue to roll down her window. When she did, one of them shouted, "Hello, beautiful. Do you and your girlfriend want to give us your phone numbers so we can give you a call sometime?"

"Like, this is not my girlfriend, she's my ugly half-sister," Rue replied. "Do you majorly think I would so hang out with a friend who looked this grody?" Her hand gestured toward Darla.

The light turned green.

"What's your telephone number?" the guy repeated.

Rue yelled out a number and sped away.

Darla's mouth fell open. "Did you just give them Bren's cell phone number?"

"You're totally not the only one who needs action," Rue retorted. "Brie will find this way funny."

"Do we know the same person?" Darla asked. "She won't find it amusing at all."

"Like, whatever! I so will. Besides, I've so got some other news."

"I can't wait to hear this."

"Later, we're totally going on a shopping spree to get some way cool girl clothes for our detective duties—"

"No way!" Darla blurted out. "I need some sleep."

88

"Like, please!" Rue swished her hand in the air. "We so need a mani-pedi since we'll be spending half our time as girls. I mean, we won't get them polished because I'm totally sure we'll have to be guys again." She clapped. "It's going to be way fun!"

"Do you realize how hung-over I am?" Darla slouched down. "And what the hell is a mani-pedi?"

"It's a manicure and pedicure, silly," Rue reacted. "You majorly need to know your female terms if you're going to be a stunning creature like me."

"Oh, Lord, give me strength."

"Like, I don't even think that HE can fix your nasty mess."

Darla glared as Rue pointed.

"I totally told you last night not to drink too much, but who didn't listen?"

"Get that out of my face," Darla growled. "I'm too battered to deal with all the, 'I told you so' crap."

"Like, whatever!" Rue dropped her finger.

After pulling up to the Davenport Detective Agency, they got out, drudged upstairs and entered their apartment.

"Brie, where are you?" Rue roared.

"Must you scream?" Darla snarled. "My head is pounding."

"Like, I vivaciously verbalized."

"I'd say you successfully screeched."

Rue tossed her head around and walked down the hallway as Darla followed. They entered Brie's bedroom and walked up to the bed.

"Come on, Brie, you totally need to get up."

"Do not call me, Brie," came the angry response.

Rue opened the curtains. "I'll so make Darla and you some brunch."

Brie popped her head out from under the covers and pulled some unruly hair from her mouth. "Brunch!" She looked at Darla. "Wow, do you look like crap."

"You look as bad as I feel!"

89

"Come on, girls..." Rue clapped her hands. "Chop! Chop! We totally need to go shopping."

"Shopping?" Brie bellowed. "You must be out of your mind. I feel like death warmed over—"

"More like scorching hot," Darla added.

"Then you must be burnt to a crisp!" Brie cackled.

"Like, you both will feel way better with a new outfit on," Rue remarked. "I so read in one of my fashion magazines that a mall experience majorly raises a girl's spirit."

"Well, my spirit needs to fall into rest," Brie grumbled.

"Oh, but wait!" Darla chimed in. "She also wants us to get something called a mani-pedi."

"Why can't we go tomorrow to get that all done?" Brie pulled the covers back over her head.

"Because, we're so picking up Lydia tonight as girls," Rue responded. "I totally told her we'd be by around 9:00pm."

"Good, then I can sleep until 8:30pm," Brie blurted out.

"Like, you two need something to wear..." Rue snatched the blanket down again. "And you're so not shoving your wretchedly huge bodies into my clothes because you'd ruin their shape."

"Excuse me, we're all the same size," Darla stated.

"Not to mention I'd never wear those strips of fabric you call a wardrobe." Brie grimaced. "I need something regal to enrich my figure."

"You mean, to way cover it up," Rue quipped.

"I mean, to enhance it," Brie growled. "I want my appearance to revere women, not demean them." She scowled. "No lady would be caught dead; let alone alive in your whore décor. It barely conceals a woman's unmentionables."

Rue glared. "It's totally about the placement."

"Then I'd place it in a trash can." Brie sneered.

"Enough ladies," Darla clamored. "We have more important issues placed before us."

90

"Totally!" Rue tossed her hair to the side. "Like, we have to go out tonight with Lydia and gossip with her. We'll get her so drunk that she doesn't go into work tomorrow—"

"And we'll also get her to tell us about Logan Price and find out what he and his cohorts are up to," Darla added.

"Slow down! I have a better idea," Brie crowed. "You go out and get her really drunk while Darla and I sleep. And if by some freak of nature you don't find out anything then we can go out the next night with her and Derek. I will be Bren and you can go as my girlfriend. Problem solved."

"Three heads are way better than one," Rue countered. "Like, she'll confide in three girls but if we go out and you two are men, she might not be so forthcoming and we majorly need a lead. Besides, she totally slept with Derek, and he—or should I say she—ran out on Lydia."

"What? Brie flung the blanket off and sat up. "You slept with her!"

"I slept, I think. Oh, I don't know what I did." Darla plopped down on the edge of the bed. "All I know is I woke up as a woman and naked, although I sometimes sleep in the nude."

Brie snickered. "That was more information than I wanted to hear."

"I know!" Darla rubbed her forehead.

"Like, were you a man or a woman when you and Lydia crawled into the sack together?" Rue asked.

"Now there's a question you don't get asked every day," Brie reacted.

Darla closed her eyes. "Let me see, from the bar to the bed, ah...I don't recall any of it." She opened them. "If I didn't have such a massive headache, I could think better."

"There's a bottle of maximum-strength Advil in the bathroom," Brie mentioned.

"Thanks!" Darla jumped up and dashed into the bathroom.

Brie's cell phone rang. She leaned over, took it off her nightstand and opened it. "Hello," her gruff voice answered.

91

"What? Who is this filthy-talking pig?" She was appalled. "You need some soap in your mouth to wash it clean." Her teeth gritted. "Where did you get my number?

Darla walked in.

"A gorgeous blonde and a sultry redhead gave it to you, huh," Brie repeated. "Well, just for future reference, this is a convent and I'm Mother Superior. Sister Sinful and Sister Sinister enjoy playing what they consider pranks," she denounced. "They will be severely chastised for their behavior."

Darla's widened eyes looked toward Rue.

"That's understandable!" Brie remarked. "Now for your part in this shenanigans, you will do me the favor of saying twenty Hail Mary's and an Act of Contrition." She hung up.

Darla and Rue turned to leave.

"I'll snatch you both back by your rosary beads if one more step is taken." Brie threw her cell phone on the nightstand. "Other than the devil, what possessed you two to do something so hateful?

They turned around.

"I, ah..." Darla faltered. "It was, um—"

"It's totally my fault," Rue admitted. "She had nothing to do with it."

Brie pointed her finger. "Don't ever do that to me again! Understand?"

Their heads nodded in agreement.

"Like, not to make any excuses, but I majorly felt overwhelmed by my feminine side and thought it would be way funny. It so backfired!"

Brie shrugged. "It's not a big deal so let's forget it."

"I already have," Darla said.

Rue breathed out. "Like, me too."

"This is all so bizarre," Brie declared. "We were exposed to some kind of solution and now have the capability to change from a man into a woman, and at our own will."

92

"Excuse me!" Rue swung her hair to the side. "You two lushes can't change back yet. Like, I'm the only one who so has her own will."

Brie snickered. "More like is so willful."

"Well, it's still crazy," Darla remarked. "Who would believe that we could fall into a liquid then change sexes?"

"I totally would," Rue answered.

"Of course!" Brie mocked. "Did I tell you the Washington Monument is up for sale and I know the broker?"

"Play nice," Darla rumbled.

"I know one thing though," Brie croaked. "I'll never drink alcohol ever again."

"Same here," Darla added. "It feels as though someone has dropped a sledgehammer on my head—repeatedly."

"Tonight, you two can way pretend to drink and when Lydia gets majorly sloshed, she might get loose with the tongue and totally expose a major clue that gives us another piece of the puzzle," Rue issued.

"Just think, Darla. If she gets drunk enough, she might expose something to you..." Brie laughed. "Or give you another piece."

"Shut up before I expose a piece of my fist!"

"Like, you both need to relax," Rue quipped.

"That's what we've been trying to tell you." Brie dropped her head back onto the pillow and pulled the blanket over it.

"What if I made a mad deal with the two of you?" Rue asked.

"We're listening," Brie said in a muffled voice.

"I'll so let you girls sleep for a while, and even make you some brunch for when you wake up—"

"I can handle that," Darla chimed in.

"Wait, I'm not finished," Rue uttered. "After we eat and take showers, we'll totally go to the mall before we pick Lydia up. Like, deal?"

"Like, deal!" Both answered simultaneously then erupted with laugher.

Rue shook her head.

When the roaring stopped, Darla asked, "Brie, have you tried changing back into a man?"

"Yes, several times," she groused, pulling the covers down to her neck. "But to no avail."

"So watch this!" Rue took off her dress and heels then stood still with her eyes closed. Within seconds, Russ appeared before them.

Darla huffed. "Put some clothes on."

"We don't want to see any of that," Brie squawked. "Especially as nauseous as I feel."

"Like, all women love seeing me in my birthday suit." Russ baited.

"Not these two," Brie remarked.

Russ pouted his lips. "Is somebody totally jealous?"

"Not even close," Brie retorted.

Darla grimaced. "Russ, stop rubbing it in our face."

"You heard her," Brie barked. "This is probably a side effect from our drinking last night. Soon, we will become men again, and when we do we'll both beat you into the ground—"

"And beyond, right into the grave," Darla added.

"So no way!" Russ grinned. "Like, the only thing being put to death is your manhood because you two are broads."

Brie snickered. "Even as broads we could still take you down."

"Way down," Darla quipped.

Both girls broke out in laughter.

"Like, whatever!" Russ scoffed. "If you two weren't major lushes you could so do this." He morphed into Rue then back into Russ.

"You are such a show-off," Darla stated.

Brie smirked. "At least put some boxers on so—"

"So hold on!" Russ morphed back into Rue. She smiled. "That's way better."

"A pair of panties and a bra would be too," Darla relayed.

94

Rue threw on her clothes. "Like, you two get your needed beauty sleep and I will totally go downstairs and tell Raymond where we're at in the case."

"Sounds awesome to me." Darla walked out.

"Close those curtains on your way out," Brie ordered.

When finished, Rue traipsed out, slid on her heels and grabbed a bag by the front door. After trotting down the stairs, she entered the detective agency and stopped at the receptionist's desk.

"Blanche, like thanks for lending me your dress." She handed over the bag.

"Did it work?"

"It totally did its job," Rue retorted. "Is Raymond in?"

"Yes, he's in his office."

Rue smiled, turned the corner and walked in.

"Hi, Raymond." She closed the door.

"Jack just called with some disturbing news. It seems that some members from the conspiracy group, ACE—"

"All Cover-ups Exposed!" Rue sat down and crossed her legs. "What is there major malfunction?"

"Well, the governor's wife took it upon herself and made arrangements to have her son transported to Passafume Funeral Parlor so he could be interred in the family mausoleum."

"Like, how icky?" Rue's face scrunched. "My moms and pops so know that I want to be cremated. Just make sure they totally turn that oven on turbo then toss me into the Pacific Ocean—urn and all!"

With his head tilted, Raymond stared at her.

"So give me the dirt on ACE."

"Supposedly, they broke into the funeral parlor, found Carlton Woodbine and took several photos of his disfigured body."

Rue's mouth fell open as her eyes expanded. "Like, no way!"

"They have been making the rounds on the Internet with the caption: **What really happened to Carlton Woodbine?** Jack is fuming, and the Woodbines are furious. Not only does he have to find

95

out who took those pictures, he has to console the First Family who should've left their son in the capable hands of Medical Examiner, Edgar Cromwell. From there, the casket could've been escorted by police to his final resting place."

"Does he totally want us to handle ACE?" Rue asked. "You know we have our own hacker upstairs with mad computer skills."

"No, Jack wants you three to stay on the case and gather all the information available so it'll be a clean bust," Raymond answered. "He doesn't want another Rutherford incident where some dirty cops stacked the case with tainted evidence. The FBI took a major hit with that mistrial."

"Like, seriously?" Rue sounded irritated. "He knows that all three of us have turned in corrupt cops, so we could what—become dirty detectives ourselves? I totally don't think so!

Raymond held up his hands. "No, *I'm* saying this," came the response. "If Derek goes on the computer and does anything to ACE, the Second Amendment Advocate Committee, or SAAC as they are known, will be all over it. And trust me, they have a brigade of computer geniuses that would make Derek look computer-illiterate!"

She exhaled. "I guess you're majorly right."

"I know I'm majorly right!" He winked.

Rue smiled. "Did you so mention our new alter egos?"

"I didn't," Raymond replied. "I wanted Jack to get through this crisis before telling him about your crisis. He needs a clear mind to comprehend this muddled catastrophe. However, I did tell him you guys were making great progress. Did I jump the gun?"

"Like, I will get to that arsenal, but first I have to tell you another item, and it's a real pistol," Rue reacted. "This morning, I majorly received a phone call from what used to be Derek. He also drank last night and so turned into a girl."

"There are now three women upstairs?"

"Totally!"

He exhaled while shaking his head "Oh, boy—"

"So what?"

96

"Three boys are one thing," Raymond responded. "Three girls on the other hand is a whole other ballgame."

"We still know how to majorly play the game," Rue remarked. "Like, just some of the rules have been changed."

"Yes, they most certainly have," Raymond added. "I had three older sisters. Trust me when I say this; they were always fighting. If it wasn't over clothing and who it belonged to, it would be over boys and who he belonged to. The sad truth was they still fought as adults and passed away hating each other."

"Like, why haven't you told us this before?

"Because I've never had three girls living together before. Especially upstairs."

"We will totally get along," Rue maintained. "Our tastes are way different."

"We'll see," he muttered. "I'll assume you've come up with female names for yourselves." Raymond grabbed a notepad and pen. "I'll need to write them down."

"I'm Rue. Bren is now Brie, and Derek, I have so named her Darla."

Raymond shook his head. "Oh, boy."

"Like, it should be...oh, girl."

"Ok, Rue, Brie and Darla," Raymond reiterated, looking down at his notepad. "As I process this new turn of events, what's going on with the case?"

"This is what we totally know so far," Rue uttered. "There's this heinous group of men who so want to use a grody chemical on a powerful man to control him."

"What do you mean by control him?"

"Like, these men are under the impression that a formula they've majorly created will change this person's feelings from a man's way of thinking into a woman's way of reasoning and feeling."

"For what reason?"

"They so discussed an old adage in the Bible that states 'a man dominates a woman and she craves his attention'..." Rue swirled out her hand. "They're such a bunch of Neanderthals."

97

"Who are these men?"

"Like, the Speaker of the House, Logan Price, is the ring-leader," she replied. "There's also a man by the name of Henry Prescott. He totally owns the chemical company where this stuff is being made. His main chemist, Buford Higgins, is making this sinister potion but can't seem to get it right. Hence the dead bodies."

"Obviously, they're not achieving the proper ratio for it to work," Raymond noted. "I have the distinct feeling there are going to be more dead bodies while it's being refined. The consequences could be staggering. Is there more?"

"Yes!" She nodded. "The next man, Arvin Horton, so runs a militia group called M.A.G.O.C., and they are all members in it. These guys are way mad at the government for all of the restrictions that are heaped upon the American people, and for their liberties being taken away. Not to mention there's some new legislation that Congress wants signed into law that the right-wing conservatives majorly hate."

"I know the world is in bad shape, but do we really need more crazies coming out of the woodwork with their distorted views?"

"Now they've so hired a woman by the name of Lydia Reome to help perfect this elixir," Rue responded. "Like, she's a French physicist, and I feel she'll way accomplish the task."

"What's your next move?"

"Me and the girls are going to take Lydia out on the town tonight and get her wickedly drunk so she won't be able to go into work tomorrow and perfect the formula," Rue replied. "We'll also pump her for information under the guise of gossip and just maybe, she'll give us the major break we need. Like, she's dating the Speaker of the House so there's plenty she must know, and in a few short hours I'll totally know."

"Good!" Raymond nodded. "I'll call Jack Stanwick and give him an update. I will also tell him what happened to you gals."

Rue got up from the chair. "Well, I'm going back upstairs to make a way delectable brunch for the girls." She headed toward the door.

"You can cook?" Raymond asked. "I mean, I know Russ couldn't."

98

"I'm so not Russ," she reacted, swinging open the door. "I'm now Rue; a totally independent woman with a few tricks up my sleeve."

Raymond's eyebrows arched. "Tricks?"

Rue winked. "Like, tricks...and treats!" The door closed behind her.

Chapter 7

As mouth-watering aromas permeated throughout the kitchen, Rue put the finishing touches on her delectable meals. After bringing them into the dining room, she placed the spread onto the table and arranged the appetizing morsels, allowing their aesthetic value to show.

Like, everything looks so delicious.

Rue walked into the living room, knelt on the couch and cracked a window. After leaning over onto the sill, she looked out onto the neighborhood and noticed the smoke rising above the nearby chimneys. A gust of autumn breeze rushed in.

Hmm, I totally love the smell of wood burning in a fireplace.

Rue raised herself from the sofa, trotted toward Brie's bedroom and opened the door. "Like, it's time to wake up!" She opened the curtains and let the light stream in.

"Must you do that?" Brie rolled over and popped her head out from under the covers. "I need more sleep."

"And I totally told you earlier that we needed to go shopping to get some clothes for tonight's festivities." Rue walked toward her. "Plus, we need to get a mani-pedi so our nails look way fabulous." She put up her hand and wiggled her fingers.

"Oh, not that again!" Brie bellowed. "My nails look good just the way they are."

"Like, whatever," Rue uttered. "We also discussed picking up Lydia and getting her wickedly drunk, so she won't be able to go into work tomorrow and perfect that heinous concoction. Not to mention we'll totally pump her for all the information, gossip and dirt she knows."

"Your brain amazes me," Brie stated. "One moment you can't remember where the refrigerator is located, but the next, you're hatching a great scheme."

"I'll so take that as a major compliment." Rue grabbed the blanket and yanked it down.

"Give me that back!" Brie blew a strand of hair away from her face then looked down. "I can't believe I'm still a woman." She huffed. "When will this go away?"

"Like, you didn't catch a common cold," Rue replied. "Besides, being able to so change from a woman back into a man is way above most doctors' pay grades."

"Well, I'm just saying it better not damage my manhood," Brie stated. "I need my piece!"

"Speaking of piece, I might've totally found one to your puzzling situation."

"Please, enlighten me."

"Like, something is telling me that alcohol is our nemesis."

Brie cocked her head.

"Totally think about it..." Rue sat down on the bed. "You and Derek so couldn't turn into women, but the moment you drank, it came to fruition. A coincidence? I think not."

"Maybe, you're right...but not being able to drink my Tanqueray and tonic with a wedge of lime is not going over well in my mind," Brie griped. "Although, if I drink one, I might possibly turn back into a man—"

"Or you could seriously stay as a woman longer."

"Must you say that?" Brie snapped. "I enjoy my maleness and want to be female-less."

"So, you're saying that being a girl is way grody?"

"Wow, you can't pull any wool over those mascara-infested eyes."

"Like, I'm just saying that being a guy has way more limitations; where being a girl has a lot to offer."

"Could you elaborate?"

101

"Being a woman has major advantages," Rue reacted. "You can totally wear your hair in a lot of different ways according to your mood." She ran her hands through her blonde curls. "You can so wear it down and tousled on one day, straight and smooth on another or up and classy on yet another. You can also have it in a ponytail, pigtails, pulled off to the side or even in tight braids."

Brie scrunched her face. "Did you just say braids?"

"Like, I'm just pointing out the many hairstyles a girl can way coordinate with whatever outfit she wears...at least that's what I've so read and seen in my fashion magazines."

"I want my hair and wardrobe to match my conservative personality."

"Then so wear your mop parted on the side and flat," Rue uttered. "Like, there must be some of those majorly boring clothes way hidden in the back of a store on clearance racks."

"Our tastes fall on opposite ends of the spectrum," Brie remarked. "You would rather look very much a slut—"

"And you would rather look totally like a mutt."

They glared at each other.

"Then there's all the make-up we can so wear," Rue mentioned. "Like, a girl can paint her face in many ways. A little mascara with a light lipstick, some fierce color on the lids with a glitzy blush, a heavy lip below soft cheeks or even thick eyeliner against a dewy complexion—"

"I want to have an all-natural look, not the face of a floozy."

Rue prattled on. "One can totally throw on a pair of jeans and a halter-top, a pretty blouse with sexy shorts, a button-down shirt tucked into a pencil skirt or even a cute mini-dress...not to mention the shoes—"

"Not to mention the cost."

"Like, you're such a major tight-wad," Rue quipped. "We make beaucoup bucks at this gig. So, stop the complaining and get your wickedly wretched rear out of bed because your tasty morsels are simmering and need to be munched on soon."

102

"Wait, hold on a moment!" Brie stuck a pinky finger in her ear and twisted it. "Let me clean this out a second." She removed it. "I could've sworn you just said that you made us something to eat."

"Don't even take me there!" Rue threw up her hand. "I so told you earlier that I was totally going to make brunch for you girls."

"Yes, but being in this awful condition and all, I thought maybe it was a hallucination. Besides, I'm so used to the McDonalds-loving Russ, I just figured you'd be no more domesticated than he was."

Rue looked into the mirror and fluffed her hair. "I majorly fooled you, didn't I?"

"Well, I guess we'll see," Brie replied. "Enlighten me, what did you prepare for our dining pleasure?"

"Like, don't get so excited," Rue stated. "It's just soup and sandwiches."

Brie laughed. "Now that's a meal that Russ would make."

"Mock all you want!" Rue waggled her finger in the air. "I was only thinking about the delicate condition your tummies are probably in from the night of cocktailing that you two lushes way engaged in. Not to mention you want to so keep those girlish figures intact."

"Well, I guess you're right—for once."

"Like, get your tired mess up out of that bed and go eat," Rue ordered. "There's a lot to do," she said. "While you girls are so slopping up your food, I'll jump into the shower."

"You're not going to eat dinner with us?"

"I way ate while I slaved over the stove."

"Slaved!" Brie sneered. "Yes, that's the word I would've used." She climbed out of bed and wrapped the blanket around her naked body. "All I have is men's clothing and I can't wear those into the mall to shop. It wouldn't look very ladylike—now would it?"

"Like, go into my bedroom and grab something that I totally bought last night when we went to the Back Alley Bar," Rue replied. "There are four pairs of heels in the bottom of my closet. Just don't stretch them out with those big grody hooves."

"Please, my feet will swim in them."

"Please, those anchors would so sink."

103

They entered Rue's bedroom. Brie walked over and rummaged through the closet. After taking an item from a hanger, she dropped her blanket, put it on and looked in the mirror. "I don't mean to sound ungrateful, especially after making us brunch, but all of your clothes are something one would see on a...let me see, for the lack of a better word or two—a call girl."

"I can majorly think of a better word or two—a cool girl. Like, way too cool! And besides that, a call girl wouldn't be able to afford my fierce clothes."

"That depends on who is calling her—"

"And how much she charges!" Darla yelled out from her bedroom.

"Like, you so need to drag your carcass up out of that crypt," Rue groused.

"All your yapping has kept me up for the last ten minutes and cut into my much needed—and I do mean needed—sack time," Darla squawked.

"Well, it's time to get up, you drunken tramp," Brie shouted. "We have to eat, shower, get dressed and pick up Lydia for a night of gossip. Doesn't that just sound like loads of fun?"

"I'd rather pluck out my right eye with a shrimp fork," Darla roared.

Rue turned and trotted out of her bedroom.

"You might want to hide that shrimp fork," Brie remarked as she followed behind.

Rue entered Darla's bedroom. "Like, it's time to get up."

"Leave me alone." She enunciated each word.

Rue marched up to the bed and yanked the blanket down. "I've majorly lived up to my end of the bargain. It's so your turn."

Darla pulled it back over her head. "I need to rest some more."

"That's way not happening!" Rue snatched it back down.

"Just give me a few more minutes," Darla pleaded.

"I so know you, babe!" Rue shot back. "Like, your few minutes will totally be a few hours and we don't have that kind of time. So, get those major boobies out of bed and come eat the brunch I made with my delicate fingers."

Darla's eyes expanded. "You made us a meal?"

"Seriously?" Rue glared. "You girls so don't listen to a word I say!"

Brie snickered. "That is true."

Darla sat up. "Nice outfit! You should go outside to the corner and make some extra money."

"At least I'm pretty enough to do it," Brie countered.

Rue shook her head. "Call it a woman's intuition, but I had a wicked feeling something like this would so happen last night if you two drank too much."

"Oh, stop your nagging," Brie snarled. "You're such a female."

"Leave her alone," Darla snapped. "You're just bitter because you feel so bad."

Brie sneered. "No, I'm much better because you look so bad!"

Rue huffed. "Like, we have a job to do, so you two totally need to step up to the plate."

"Yes, the dinner plate," Brie added.

Darla got out of bed. "Damn, I'm in no mood for this."

"Grin and bear it, dear," Brie uttered. "Sometimes a woman has to do things when she is not in the mood."

"I'm sure," Darla grumbled. "I'm just not one of them."

"Come, follow me," Brie stated. "I have picked out the perfect outfit for you."

"What does it look like?" Darla asked.

"Let's just say it's not as conservative as mine," Brie replied.

"Well, I need to wear it out in public," Darla noted.

"Just don't stand too long on the street or its corner," Brie remarked. "Besides, no matter how tawdry it looks, Rue's outfit will have it beat."

"And what does that totally mean?"

Brie shrugged. "Absolutely nothing."

105

"Like, whatever!" Rue smirked. "I'm taking a quick shower then trotting across the street to Chisholm's Drugstore to buy some makeup, hair brushes and a couple of snazzy blow dryers. I so placed a fashion magazine under each of your plates, that way you can majorly look at the latest makeup tips while you eat."

Brie scoffed. "How hard can it be to put on makeup?"

"I know, right?" Darla retorted.

"I mean, look how quickly you took to it," Brie commented. "If you can do it, we certainly will have no problem."

"I totally feel that wasn't a compliment." Rue's eyes glared.

Brie smiled. "Well, if the shoe fits—"

"I'll so take one off and beam it at you!" Rue reached down.

"Now that's not a feminine gesture," Brie claimed.

Rue lifted her hand. "Like, neither is this—"

Darla grabbed her wrist and interrupted the oncoming salute. "That's not for a pretty girl to do." She flung her hand up and flipped the bird. "It's more for a tomboy."

"Oh, please," Brie hissed.

Rue turned and headed off to the bathroom.

Brie took off the dress and wrapped herself up with the blanket. "I'm hungry."

"I hear you," Darla added.

"We can look for something to wear later," Brie said.

Darla nodded. "Yeah, much later.

They both laughed.

Brie walked out of the bedroom and toward the dining room.

Darla tagged behind then bypassed her and entered the kitchen.

"Will you grab the mustard?" Brie sat down and opened up a fashion magazine.

"I've got two soup bowls to bring in," Darla answered. "What would you like me to do with it? Balance it on my head."

"Please."

"Anything else you want, your highness?"

"I will let you know, your hind-ass."

Darla brought the soup in, placed it on the table then fetched the mustard. She sat down and picked up her spoon. "I hope it's delicious."

Brie looked up from the magazine. "Rue made it, so it will barely taste adequate."

Darla scooped up a spoonful and put it into her mouth. "It's not half bad."

"Then it's only half good," Brie countered.

Darla chuckled. "Taste it."

"I will as soon as I peruse this article."

"What's it about?"

"Listen to this, 'Are Pantyhose Dead?' That's the caption—"

"Read it out loud."

"If I must." Brie exhaled. "Women have walked from the last century into the new millennium leaving behind the once garnered item that their mothers and grandmothers never left home without. It is the pantyhose. More and more women are shunning this beloved artifact for an easier alternative. Whether sprayed on, bronzer-applied or machine-procured, it seems like nude is the way to go. A poll from women ages 25-45 exposed a surprising trend; 92% of them don't wear pantyhose. Most companies have seen a steep decline over the last fifteen years in the sales of the leg-veiling product. It seems society is embracing the leg and even promoting its beauty. From the skyrocketing sales of various hair-removing, moisturizing and exfoliating products, the leg is coming out in all its glory. Even in the business realm, more and more women are being seen in shorter skirts with barren legs. Maybe soon, the only place one might see a pair of pantyhose could be in the ever-expanding Smithsonian." She focused on Darla. "Would you wear them?"

"No, that's definitely not my thing." Her head shook. "Why, would you?"

"It would depend on the situation."

107

"You'd probably wear them to one of those snazzy social gatherings your parents have attended."

"If I received an invitation to the White House then a pair would be worn—"

Darla slurped a spoonful of soup.

"My mother would always complain about them. I remember her exact words. 'These stockings seem to get a run in them the minute I open a new pair. For heaven's sakes, you would think I was doing calisthenics in them.' I always thought that was quite funny."

"My mom hardly ever wore a dress, except for special occasions," Darla recalled. "That's the only time I've seen her in them."

"My mother always wore dresses; even to get the mail," Brie admitted as she picked up her sandwich.

Some time had passed when Rue came into the dining room. Although dressed, her hair remained damp.

"Is that your idea of a quick shower?" Brie asked.

"I so rushed," Rue reacted. "Like, I normally take twice as long. Half of that time is just for shampooing and conditioning my hair which is way thick and curly."

"If it takes that long, you should cut some of that nappy mess off instead of cutting into our shower time," Brie stressed. "Darla will now have to rush."

"Me?"

"Of course!" Brie bellowed. "You cannot expect that of me. I am much more hygienic than you."

Darla winced. "Really?"

"Like, I know what will save time," Rue suggested. "You both can totally take one together."

"What?" Brie balked. "I don't want to shower with that filthy mess."

"Yeah, I'm not taking one with that dirty wreck either," Darla declared.

108

Rue folded her arms. "Like, we won't be able to browse at the stores if you don't."

"Blackmail!" Brie blurted out. "Why must I suffer for your lollygagging?"

"And suffer she will," Darla uttered. "It takes Bren two hours to buy one polo shirt. What's it going to be like now that she's a girl?"

"It will be dry clean only for me," Brie retorted. "I'm not the wash and wear type."

"But you'll wear a washcloth and wash my back, won't you?" Darla requested.

Brie's eyes narrowed.

"What?" Darla shrugged. "It's really hard to get that area. Since you're going to be in there anyways, I might as well use you."

"Like, everybody else has!" Rue giggled.

Brie gritted her teeth.

"That's so my cue to leave." Rue grabbed her purse, slid on her heels and opened the door. "Don't forget to totally look at those beauty tips."

"Why, they haven't worked for you?" Brie quipped.

Rue stuck out her tongue then closed the door.

"Well, that meal hit the spot." Darla started clearing the table. "After I put these dishes in the sink, I'm getting into the shower."

"I'll be there in a moment." Brie's head stayed buried in the magazine. "I want to finish this other article."

"I wouldn't dillydally," Darla remarked. "Rue will be back soon, and you know what she'll be like if you're not on schedule. Do you want to deal with her the way you feel? I don't."

"I don't either!" She closed the magazine and tossed it aside. After getting up from the table, Brie walked toward the bathroom with Darla in tow. Once inside, they undressed and got into the shower. Water gushed from above.

"It's hot!"

"Stop your whining." Brie grasped the bar of soap and lathered up her body.

109

"Could you move out of my way?"

"Watch it," Brie barked. "You almost knocked me over."

"Then give me some room, you big sow."

"Who are you calling a sow?"

Shampoo dripped down Darla's face. "Ah, duh!"

"I'd watch my tongue if I were you."

"Really?" Darla baited. "Or what?"

"You don't want me to answer that."

"Oh, but I do!"

"Don't push me," Brie snarled.

"Just remember, you could find your fat, suds-ridden ass feeling some tile."

"Just remember, your equally large backside could be experiencing it too."

"Wouldn't that be a pretty sight?" Darla rinsed her hair. "I'd love to see the expression on Rue's face if she walked in with you and I wrestling wet and naked on the floor."

"She would be livid."

"Right."

They busted out with laughter.

"What do you think about Rue?" Darla asked.

"Other than her being an utter nuisance—"

"I mean, her preparing us dinner." Darla slathered conditioner through her hair. "That was really cool."

"She is also letting us borrow her clothes and shoes."

"Rue has somehow tapped into the domesticated goddess lobe of her brain—"

"Or she just really wants to go shopping." Brie stated "Time will tell."

"Well, I'm giving her the benefit of the doubt."

"Do you want to hear me say something crazy?"

110

Darla gripped onto the bar of soap. "And how's that different from any other time?"

"I'm being serious!"

"Then go ahead and be serious."

"I feel Rue has really stepped up to the plate." Brie reached for the shampoo bottle. "I mean, she came up with this great plan for tonight, which is usually my department, being that I'm the smart one. She made brunch for us, which you usually do because you're the domesticated one, and because nobody else will do it." She foamed up her hair. "I always assumed Russ was the pretty one who would get by on his laurels, but now being Rue, she seems to have taken it to another level."

Darla pushed aside the shower curtain. "I've never counted her out." She grabbed a towel, put it around herself and stepped out.

"I can't believe you've finished showering already. I figured you'd be much dirtier from your night with Lydia."

"Oh, you do want to end up on the floor."

"If that happens, I'm taking you with me."

"I'm going to let some of this steam out." Darla swung open the bathroom door. "Oh, boy, here comes Rue."

"I thought we got rid of her for a while," Brie stated. "I mean, it took her almost an hour just to get her slathering tongue back into her mouth the night we stopped and shopped for women's clothes at that designer boutique. I thought the shop girl was going to take out a restraining order—"

"Or be required to go to Shopaholics Anonymous," Darla added. "She must possess the ability to smell what she needs a block away, zero in on it then swoop down for the kill."

Rue stood in the doorway. "Like, what did you girls kill?"

"The sexual grime on Darla," Brie responded. "Well, it wasn't so much killed as it was scrubbed asunder."

"So was her reputation," Rue quipped.

"That's definitely down the drain!" Brie chuckled. "She is the first of us girls to have a female on female escapade."

111

"No way!" Darla yelled. "Russ has been with two girls at once more times that I care to count."

"As a man," Brie announced.

"I liked it better when you two hated each other and fought," Darla remarked.

"Don't worry, something irritating will fly out of her mouth soon enough," Brie declared. "When that happens, you can go back to being the mediator."

"I'm totally glad we got that out of the way." Rue turned around. "Like, I'm going to remove the items I bought from their packages and so bring them in for you girls to use."

"I can handle that!" Darla chimed in.

"Let me so call Lydia first to make sure everything is majorly on for tonight," Rue uttered.

Brie leaned out of the bathroom. "May we use some of the moisturizer you got last night?"

"Totally," Rue replied. "Like, it's the good stuff so you only need a dab." She turned around and walked over to the couch. After plopping down, she picked up the phone, popped it on speaker and dialed a number.

"The Alabaster Hotel," a woman said. "How may I assist you?"

"Like, may I please have room 604?" Rue pulled a package out of the shopping bag.

"Hello?"

"Lydia?"

"Yes."

"Like, it's Rue Munroe; the girl you met last night at the Back Alley Bar."

"How are you doing?"

"I'm totally good, and you?"

"I am fine!" Lydia answered. "Are we still on for tonight?"

"We are majorly on!" Rue smiled. "There are two girls coming out with us. We'll way pick you up around 10:00pm." She ran her fingers along the bristles of a brush. "Like, the club's right up the street from your hotel."

"Great, we will have a blast," Lydia said. "Are you dressing up or going casual?"

"I'm way wearing a wicked black bustier mini-dress that ties up the back." Rue ripped open a box. "I've also got a pair of fierce heels that tie around the ankles." She took out a blow dryer. "What are you so wearing?"

"I have a beautiful gold cocktail dress with lace all around the bustline," Lydia answered. "It shows a peek of cleavage to preserve its classiness."

"Like, we'll look gnarly." Rue giggled.

"I do not want to stay out too late because I have to be at work early tomorrow morning, and I want to make a good first impression."

"Totally!" Rue expressed. "Just let us know when you so want to leave."

"Thank you, it should be such fun."

"Washington, DC, is way known for its night life."

"Splendid! I need a night life."

"Like, didn't you have a fun night with that guy, um...Derek?" Rue asked. "How did your night go?"

"I do not remember," Lydia replied. "I had too much to drink."

"How did you totally get back to the hotel?"

"It is a mystery."

"It's one we'll so have to solve," Rue proclaimed.

"I would rather not."

"Like, don't you want to know what majorly happened?"

"It should stay where it is; in my blackout."

"That's way cool," Rue declared. "I'll so see you around 10:00pm."

"I shall be ready," Lydia said. "Goodbye."

Rue hung up then brought the empty packages to the garbage can and threw them out. She walked to the couch to collect the items and

113

brought them to the bathroom sink where Brie and Darla stood. Both were applying moisturizer to their faces.

"Like, here you go, girls." She gave them the items. "I majorly bought two blow-dryers and an assortment of brushes, but the makeup..." Her hand went up. "Let's just say, it so wasn't Maybelline. You two can totally go to the mall bare-faced until we get the good stuff."

"That was my plan all along," Brie stated. "I wouldn't clog my pores with all of those chemicals. I'm a fresh, all-natural girl."

"You're so fresh you have an expiration date." Rue smiled. "It's too bad it way expired a month ago!"

"Listen to the girl who is full of preservatives," Brie remarked. "They could dig you up three centuries from now and you'd still look the same, albeit pastier."

Rue smirked. "Like, jealously is an ugly thing, and so are you in anything fitted."

Brie grimaced at her in the mirror. "In a moment, my foot is to be fitted up your—"

"Ok, enough!" Darla interrupted. "I thought we were on a tight schedule."

"We totally are," Rue uttered. "So let's get the show on the road!

Brie huffed. "I still need to get dressed—"

"And my hair is still wet," Darla griped.

Rue glared at both of them. "Like, you girls need to stop the bitching and get yourselves bewitching!"

Chapter 8

The atmosphere was extremely energetic as employees scrambled to get their articles in before the dreaded deadline. Simone handed in her editorial item before the hustle and bustle advanced. She prided herself on keeping pace and not allowing outside influences to disturb her work.

"Hello, Ms. Wellington?" The receptionist rang in.

"Yes!"

"You have a call on line three."

"Do you know who it is?" Simone asked.

"The man would not give his name, but asked to speak with you right away. It sounded urgent."

Maybe, it's Jack. She smiled. "Ruth, put him through, please."

"Yes, Ms. Wellington."

When the blinking red light appeared, Simone pushed it. "Hello." She beamed.

There was silence.

"Ah...hello?"

She heard heavy breathing on the other end.

"Jack, is that you?"

"Um...no, ah...it's not."

This man has a heavy drawl.

"Hello, Miss Wellington?"

115

"This is Ms. Wellington." Her face glowered. "To whom am I speaking?"

"Ms. Wellington, I'm calling to invite you—"

"Invite me where?" Her voice reared.

"To an exclusive interview regarding the green technology program we've instituted at our chemical plant."

I know this voice. It's that Buford Higgins. I'm going to hang up. No, wait! Jack wanted me to be nice and to get all of the information I can out of him. I need to keep him talking.

Simone looked at the contraption that was installed on her phone.

I need to push down this button here. Her finger lingered. *If I do that, Jack will still not have the information he needs to apprehend this guy. I should see what this is about. An interview would allow me to get up close and personal. I can get close to Buford where Jack can't. At least, not like I can. That's it! I'll ask him some leading questions. Maybe he'll say something incriminating. Yes, I'll use my feminine wiles to get the information Jack needs. I can't push this button!*

"Ms. Wellington, are you still there?"

"Yes, I'm still here." Her tone pleasant. "Please, tell me more."

"Ah...ok. I'm the lead chemist for Prescott Chemicals in Norgerville, Virginia. I've been spearheading the creation of an environmentally-safe pesticide. It will exterminate 99.9% of the crop-destroying insects on our planet. The formula is completely green. It's made from organic materials found in nature and will not harm humans or livestock. I called you first to give an exclusive interview before we launch it next week to the media. Are you interested?"

"Of course," Simone reacted. "May I ask a question?"

"Sure."

"Why did you choose me?"

"Um...ah—"

"I don't mean to sound ungrateful. This is a great opportunity. I guess I'm just wondering why me?"

116

"Ah..." He cleared his throat. "It's just that, um...I read your articles every morning, and I, ah...I felt you would be the best journalist to write an objective story about us and our product."

"Oh, thank you," Simone uttered. "I really do try to be unbiased and report the facts without any opinions."

"That's the reason I want you to do the interview."

"When and where will this interview take place?

"It'll be tomorrow; 8:00am at Prescott Chemicals."

"Tomorrow?"

"Is there a problem?"

"No!"

"This'll be the only chance to get the full story about our revolutionary product before it's announced to the world."

"And I'll be the only one covering it?"

"It'll be only you."

He's up to something, but all in all, I need to do this for Jack. Simone inhaled. "Tomorrow, it is."

"You won't regret it."

I hope I don't. Simone gulped. "Before our conversation ends, may I ask you a personal question?"

"Um...ah, sure."

"Are you Buford Higgins?"

Simone heard him gasp.

"Please, don't hang up," she pleaded. "Are you there?"

He said nothing.

Shoot! I've lost him.

"Yeah, um...I'm here."

Simone exhaled.

"How did you know it was me?"

"It was your easy southern lilt that gave you away."

"Huh?"

117

"The only reason for asking was to find out if I was coming down tomorrow to interview you."

"Ah, you were?" Buford uttered. "Yeah, it's with me."

"Good, I was hoping we would meet again."

"You did?"

"When you stopped calling me I figured you weren't interested anymore."

"You wouldn't accept my calls so I thought you were avoiding me."

"No!" Her face scrunched. "I was just so busy, especially after the Jonestown Massacres." *It's a little white lie time.* "Then I was sent overseas to cover the 20th anniversary of the Soviet Union's invasion of Afghanistan, which unfortunately started the Cold War. I was there a while."

"I was just talking about our trip to Guyana with my colleague and about seeing you there."

It's time to reel him in. "I was glad we met."

"You were?"

"Yes, your curiosity inspired me."

"It did?"

"Of course!" *This lie is becoming darker.* "From my point of view, you were a kind and respectful gentleman."

"Then why didn't you go out to supper with me when I asked?"

"The only reason I declined your dinner invitation was because I had been sent there on a business assignment and thought my going out with you would be considered unprofessional," Simone answered. "Not to mention being new at journalism and wanting to impress my boss, I took my notes during the day and stayed up late every night putting all the words together on paper. It just couldn't be good, it had to be great. You can see where my head was at."

"Yeah, I do."

"Unfortunately, I regretted that decision."

"Why, what for?"

118

"For missing out on the chance of getting to know a really nice guy."

"You still can, you know."

"You're quite right!" *You're so wrong!* "I don't mean to change the subject, but I wanted to know if you had a few more minutes to talk?"

"Sure, take as long as you need."

"I wanted to ask a few questions to get the cursory part of the interview over. That way when I'm down there, we can talk freely about other matters. But if you're not comfortable with me—"

"No, it's ok. I'm on a break so we can talk now."

He took that bait along with my hook, line and sinker. "Then I'll get right to it," Simone stated. "How did you come up with the inspiration for your new product?"

"Ah...I, um—"

Maybe, I should take this in another direction. "Let's wait on the interview questions until tomorrow. Together, we'll blow through them in no time."

"Oh...ok."

"May I ask you something else?"

"Go ahead."

"Anything you say here will not appear in my article whatsoever," she remarked. "I'm not writing any of this down."

"Isn't that what you call in the newspaper business—off the record?"

"Yes, you know the business."

"I read a lot, and since we get the Washington Tribune here in Virginia, I get to see all your articles," Buford said. "I even call to say how much I enjoy them in the comments section."

"Well, thank you. That'll help me keep my job."

"I hope so."

"So, when you left Guyana on your expedition to the Amazon rainforest, did you find what you were looking for?"

119

"Off the record—my boss, Henry Prescott and I flew down to the Amazon rainforest on the knowledge there was a tribe of people who were using natural substances on their crops that mimicked a pesticide. After our arrival, we took a guided excursion and located this tribe. They showed us a natural formula that kept numerous insects from destroying their crop source. Both of us knew we had to cash in on it so we asked if they could show us what was used. A couple of tribesmen brought us deep into the forest where these items were located, and once they left we gathered a load of samples, took them back to our tent and properly stored them."

"Were you given instructions on how much of each item was needed to achieve the correct results?"

"Nope. The tribesmen spoke to one another in clacks, clicks and clunks. Not a word of any language was used. Even our guide had trouble understanding them. He mostly used various hand gestures to communicate. Henry was getting hot under the collar. But they finally grasped what we were looking for."

"Wow, that was eighteen years ago..." Simone pointed out. "And you're just now bringing it to market—"

"I worked on this project alone," Buford blurted out. "Most companies have a team, but Henry didn't want anybody to know about it—"

"I'm sorry if I angered you, that wasn't my intent."

"No, you didn't," he continued. "I'm just blowing off some steam. It brought back to mind all the countless nights and weekends I worked. There was numerous cuttings that needed to grow because many a trial and error occurred. Not to mention the crops that were destroyed. My back was numb from all the seeds that needed planting. Two seasons in a row, so many tomato plants died by my various concoctions, I thought for sure that the Heinz Ketchup company would've gone out of business. Now I finally get to reap the benefits instead of being the vegetable Grim Reaper."

"My woman's intuition is telling me there's something else you're not telling me."

The connection went cold.

"Or am I wrong?"

"I can't say you'd be wrong," came his reply.

"But you're not at liberty to discuss it with me, right?"

His throated cleared. "This is still off the record, right?"

"Yes, of course. Just consider it as two friends talking about a past experience." *I'll get him to spill his guts if it's the last thing I do. Even if I have to go to dinner with him, I'll get it.*

"Ok," he said. "Later that evening, we ate dinner then got ready for bed. Sometime during the night we were woken up by a noise, a drumming of sorts. Henry and I got up, went to our guide's tent and asked what was going on. He told us there was a tribe of Mayapo natives who would occasionally perform their rituals at night and not to worry, we weren't in any danger. We went back to bed but the drumming continued, and since we couldn't sleep, Henry asked me if we should sneak into the jungle to watch what was taking place."

Ply him with reassurance. "You're really brave."

"Yeah, I was really bold back then."

Now you're a boldfaced liar, thief and most likely a murderer! "So what happened next?"

"With only a penlight, Henry and I left our tent to scope out the situation. We followed the drumbeats as they got louder. After a mile or so of walking we found the scene, hid behind some bushes and as quiet as mice we watched what happened next. It was the most incredible thing I'd ever seen."

"What was it?" Simone asked. "What did you see?"

"I probably shouldn't tell you anymore. I could get into a heap of trouble."

You're a woman; bring him around. "Now that I am interested in you and your life, you take it away from me. I feel you're not interested in me anymore."

"You're wrong."

"Then prove me right."

Buford breathed out. "We looked on as a horde of women surrounded a group of young boys who were no more than eleven or twelve years old. They were dragged to a big, black cauldron-type of pot that was cooking over an open fire. A hulking woman spooned the brewing solution into a tiny handmade cup then another equally-sized woman made each boy drink from it. We watched with awe.

Within a few seconds, these budding males turned into females. I nearly fell to the ground."

Simone gasped, cupping a hand over her mouth.

"It was shocking and amazing all at the same time. Henry turned to me with widened eyes and an even wider mouth, which is rather amazing in its own right because he can certainly yell at the top of his lungs. But not a word uttered forth. Anyhow, we held it together and focused on what was happening—"

"That's such an incredible feat!"

"Yeah, and when it was finally over, they went into what looked like huts then everything was quiet, at which point Henry looked at me and said he wanted to confiscate some of the solution. So we trekked back to our tent, took all industrial thermoses and poured out the remainder of our coffee. The two of us crept toward their encampment, tiptoed in and grabbed the potion. After that, we came back to the United States, snuck it through customs and brought it to Prescott Chemicals where it has been on liquid nitrogen to stop it from degrading."

This guy must be off his rocker. "Wow, what a story!"

"It's all true."

"I have no doubt," Simone remarked. "Your bravery amazes me. I'd have been so petrified to pull off that caper."

"Ah, it was nothing."

"I think it's something."

"You should see what we're working on now."

"What is it?"

"Um...I, ah...shouldn't have brought it up."

"Why?"

"Just forget about it."

She balked. "You can confide in me."

"By telling you, I could get myself a heap of pain."

"But look at what you might gain?"

"Huh—"

122

"I just love a good story," Simone stated.

"Um...ah, ok..." She heard him exhale. "You recently wrote about the disappearance of Carlton Woodbine."

"Yes."

"Where did you get the information?"

Simone hesitated. "A source. Why?"

"That anonymous source was me."

I knew that! She gloated. "I thought it might be you."

"I wanted to help you out."

"Wait!" Simone jerked forward. "Please, say you didn't kidnap and kill him for me?" Her voice lowered.

"No, not at all! He was an unfortunate casualty of our experiment."

"What experiment?"

"Didn't you dig further into Carlton's death?"

"I was asked to back off the story until it was solved."

"Simone, I gave you a neatly-wrapped present when I told you about the Governor of Virginia's son. All you had to do was open it."

"Buford, your gift was ripped out of my hands before I had a chance to remove the bow."

"Then you'll take this package out of a brown paper bag."

"Please, give it to me. I'll keep it for myself!"

"First, I need to ask you a question..." There was a moment of silence. "Are you a Democrat or a Republican?"

He asked me if I was a Democrat first and a Republican second. I remember an article I wrote on subliminal advertising. Usually, a person will go with the last word heard. Buford is intelligent, but he's not smart. I will go with my third choice. "I'm an Independent. There are issues on both sides of the aisle that I want to see instituted."

Another round of silence ensued.

Did he hang up?

"I'm tired of the charade." Buford cleared his throat. "I'm willing to tell you because you're working with the FBI."

123

"Who told you that?"

"I have my sources too."

"So what does the FBI have to do with it?"

"If I tell you the truth about everything then maybe I would get some leniency. I know that the FBI is handling the case, and I was hoping you could say something on my behalf."

"I'll see what can be done, but I'm not making any promises."

"All I ask is that you give me a fair shot."

"I pride myself on being impartial."

"We've been holding onto the stolen formula for years just waiting for the right time. It's now the right time," Buford proclaimed. "Congress has legislation in front of the President of the United States which will favor liberal ideals. We can't have that type of thinking in the White House or anywhere else for that fact. We're part of a right-wing group of conservative minds. With all of this left-wing rioting going on over democracy and where our tax dollars should be spent, the Republican agenda is being stripped away along with our way of life. The Democrats have been trampling on our rights and chipping away at our moral block. The gun laws are shooting the Constitution to pieces and the legalization of drugs will fill young minds while abortion takes even younger ones away. Gay marriage is killing religion, and now the taxing of faith-based institutions will be their fatal blow. We can't accept any more of this crap." There was a pause. "Don't you agree?"

I'm a Democrat and will defend my decision to the death, but today, I know what needs to be said. "I definitely agree!"

"Great!"

"How're you going to convince the President of your viewpoint?" she asked.

"The art of persuasion will come in a little glass vial."

"I'm sorry," she said. "I don't understand what that means."

"When we dose the President with our special elixir, just his feelings will be altered. It will leave his body intact."

She recoiled, nearly dropping the phone. "I thought that formula you took completely changed a boy into a girl?"

"Yeah, the one we stole from the Mayapo natives did."

"What are you saying? Did you alter the old formula? Please, correct me if I'm wrong."

"Let's just say, it required an overhaul," he replied. "I needed a substantial quantity of synthetic materials for such a small amount of formula. We brought four industrial-sized thermoses of coffee because those expeditions were known to be grueling and we'd need the caffeine for energy. Hiking through deep brush and thick woods was not an easy task. Now what I'm going to tell you next will either astound or repulse you."

I'm way past repulsion. "Go ahead."

"I performed several revisions to get it perfected. There are three partially-morphed bodies lying in the Capital's morgue. All have the same body type. One of them is Carlton Woodbine; better known as the Governor of Virginia's son. He and his wife had a closed casket, so they could put to rest the real truth. Believe me, we had no idea it was their son. I had to modify the concoction after every death to get the correct formulation. The height to weight ratio was the most challenging, but now it should work faultlessly on the President's emotional abilities."

Simone cringed as a shiver went down her spine. "By what mode will the formula be dispensed into the President's body?"

"He only has to drink one measured amount for it to work. After that, he'll be plied with compliments and doted on but at the same time, he'll be told what to do. You have to dominate the female psyche with the will of a male. That way, we'll ensure our Republican ideals. How does that sound?"

Like a male chauvinist pig! "It sounds well thought-out." *I despise this man.* "Are you the master puppeteer pulling the strings?"

"No," he replied. "That would be the Speaker of the House, Logan Price. He wants to take over the Presidency and will do everything within his power to achieve it."

Her eyebrows creased. "Isn't he a Democrat?"

"Yeah, on the outside," Buford retorted. "On the inside, he's full Republican."

125

Oh, he's full of something! "Besides your friend, Henry, who else is helping you?"

"Arvin Horton, the founder of M.A.G.O.C. We had a fifth, Harvey Welch, but he didn't end up working out. Logan didn't trust him for some reason."

"Aren't you afraid he'll talk?"

"It's a long-distance call from Hell, and we won't accept the charges."

"You mean he's dead—"

"Colder than ice," Buford quipped. "He shouldn't have become a liability."

What a barbarian! Simone wrote it down on her notepad and underlined the words three times. "Earlier, you mentioned something about M.A.G.O.C. What is it?"

"It stands for—Men Against Government Overtaking Control. It's a militia group whose motto and main purpose is to ensure the Republican way of life."

"I see."

"Are you freaked out?"

"No, not really." *Just let it roll of your back.* "However, I am quite curious about the appearance of the victims. Do you have any photographs of your handy work?"

"Didn't you see the ACE website? They showed Carlton Woodbine naked on the slab."

She breathed in then out. "All Cover-Ups Exposed was conveniently taken down."

"Oh, then I will tell you about them," he stated. "When we injected the men with our formula, they turned into half-males/half-females and died with part of their faces and bodies merged into both sexes. After that happened, we would drive to a remote spot, drop the body off and beat feet out of there. Since everybody wore gloves, when we got to Prescott Chemicals, we scrubbed the interior of the van clean. Any and all residue was burnt in the incinerator, including what was on our backs. We always kept spare clothes and shoes at the plant. I've lost a few good pairs of sneakers doing this job."

"I bet you have." *I bet you'll lose much more when the truth comes out.*

"I'm sure the police and the FBI were freaked out by what they saw. Wish I could've been a fly hovering above to see the looks on their faces when they took a gander at those crime scenes."

"I'm sure they were quite surprised."

"Oh, that they were."

"So with each death, the formula was made better," Simone noted.

"Yeah, I had to titrate my computations to augment the effect."

"I'm sorry, but I didn't understand a word you just said." *What's he speaking in Swahili?*

"This will clear it up," Buford remarked. "When we grabbed the first guy and injected him, he turned into a male/female pretty fast but then died, so I went back to the lab and amended it. The second guy, it took him a little longer, so I realized the formula was heading in the right direction. Again, I went back and adjusted it. With number three, I thought for sure it was ready, but at the very last moment he also morphed and died. So once again, I went back to the lab and gave the formula what I felt was the correct amount of tweaking, thus achieving the desired result. This time, I'm sure it will work, but to be on the safe side we're going out for one more rendezvous."

Simone's eyes widened. "When will that be?"

"If all goes well, it'll be tomorrow night," he replied. "I've got somebody coming on board in the morning to make sure it's ready for the final run."

"Did you happen to name your formula?"

"For all technical purposes, we refer to it as TB4711."

"Why did you assign it that code?"

"The two letters stand for Tonetta Biegan," Buford responded. "They're the initials of Henry's deceased wife. He used her maiden name. The numbers are for her birthday which was the seventh of April. The eleven represents the day they were married. She was sick for quite some time."

"If you don't mind me asking, what was her illness?"

127

"She was diagnosed with amyloidosis of the kidneys and had dialysis for the last few years, but never got any better. Toward the end, the doctor loaded her with morphine. It barely touched her pain."

Simone sighed. "Oh, that poor woman."

"I felt for Henry. He suffered right along with her. So when he asked me to end her life, I couldn't say no."

"What did you do?"

"I prepared a lethal enema, and when she finally fell asleep, I dosed her. She was gone in under a minute."

"Wouldn't the medical examiner know she was murdered?"

"I refer to it as an assisted suicide," Buford retorted. "Besides, he's a close friend of ours and knew what was being done."

"How long were they together?"

"It would've been fifty years this past December, but she was relieved of her fleshly duties two months shy. Henry couldn't bear the thought of making her suffer for a date on the calendar."

"That's absolutely heartrending!"

"Yeah, it's definitely tragic."

"On that sad note, I should wrap this up until tomorrow morning."

"Ok. I hope I didn't scare you away?"

"I'm a journalist," Simone expounded. "I've heard every story out there so I don't scare easily."

"True."

"I do have a very big favor to ask."

"Sure, anything you want."

"If I was to give you a very small camera, say in a ball-point pen, would you tape the entire process of the man morphing into a partial woman?" Simone asked. "All you have to do is wear a shirt with a pocket—"

"I have plenty of T-shirts with them."

128

That's not surprising! Once the cap is twisted, attach it to the inside of your pocket. That will allow an inch or more to protrude. You have about an hour's worth of tape to capture the event."

"Um...ok. Yeah, why not, I'll do it."

"You will!" she uttered. "Oh, thank you. This will help my career in so many ways. I wish I could do more to help you out."

"You could. Um...I mean, ah...would you have supper with me tomorrow night?"

"Oh...ah, as tempting as that sounds, ah...I've got to get back to Washington, DC. Yes, our interview has to get into the evening paper. I have to meet that dreaded deadline."

"What about lunch? That should give you plenty of time to meet your deadline."

"Ah...again, I'll have to see. I have many more questions about your green technology, and I will need to know everything if I'm going to have a newsworthy article."

"I've got an even better idea," he commented. "Why don't you come down this evening? Prescott Chemicals will put you up at a hotel. That way, I can take you to supper; maybe even squeeze in a movie afterwards. It'll break the ice for tomorrow's interview."

"Oh, I wish I could," Simone countered. "I've already made plans to meet a friend for drinks and dinner."

"Is it a male friend?"

It's really none of your business. "It's one of my girlfriends; an old colleague of mine. I've been telling her for weeks we'd get together so I can't stiff her. She would be really upset with me."

"Yeah, I get it."

"I knew you would understand," she said. "I'll see you tomorrow."

"8:00am sharp," Buford blurted out.

"8:00am sharp!" Simone hung up the phone and shuddered in disgust.

Chapter 9

The sprawling Yingertown Mall rested on an old agricultural spread in the farming town of Lysander, just over the Virginia state line. With its reputation of being the largest indoor shopping destination on the eastern seaboard, customers were able to avoid the hustle and bustle consuming the Capitol.

After pulling onto the main road surrounding the massive complex, Brie drove down into the underground parking garage and pulled into a vacant spot.

"Now remember, we're just picking up a few things," she said, turning her head toward the backseat. "We're not here to enter a shopping marathon. Do we understand?"

"Like, why are you looking at me?" Rue asked.

"Oh, I wonder," Brie responded.

"We can totally stay here for a while since I rushed you wretched hags," Rue uttered. "I so told Lydia to be ready by 10:00pm—"

"Who are you calling hags?" Brie snarled.

"You mean, I could've slept an extra hour," Darla squawked, swinging open the car door.

Rue got out as Brie followed suit.

Not a word was exchanged as they walked through the entrance.

"Where should we start?" Darla had a hand on her hip.

"We discussed that on the way here." Brie huffed.

"Well, with all of the arguing that went on in the car over what stores we were hitting, I don't quite remember the actual decision," Darla stated. "Not to mention I'm sleep deprived."

"I'm totally sorry—"

"Save it!" Up went Darla's hand.

A group of guys walked by and leered at them. One winked at Rue. "Wow, you're gorgeous!" His smooth voice said. "What's your name?"

She smiled. "Like, I'm—"

"Down girl," Brie growled. "You're not here to buy that." She turned to the guys. "Listen boys, it's time for you to move on."

"Aw, man," the guy whined. "Can I at least get her number?"

Brie shook her head. "Sorry, she doesn't play the numbers—"

"Besides, her number is almost up," Darla blurted out. "Now skedaddle!"

The guys displayed some down-hearted looks and walked away.

"You both need to be way nicer." Rue admonished. "Like, no man will ever ask either of you out on a date with such grody attitudes."

"That's the idea," Brie quipped.

"C'mon girls, tick tock; times a-wasting," Darla remarked.

Brie turned. "Let's go to Macy's."

"Like, I don't think so!" Rue shuddered. "That's where grannies go to shop." She pursed her lips. "I want to majorly hit Forever 21, where the clothes are young and hip...not to mention short, tight and sexy."

"Well, I want a wardrobe that is conservative," Brie countered. "Something that a lady would wear, and I don't mean a lady of the evening as in your taste."

"Are you totally serious?" Rue clamored. "Like, you're young—well sort of—and you should be wearing hot clothes. You can so wear that old crap when you're old and look like crap."

"Conservative clothes are very stylish," Brie said in her condescending tone. "There are many men who think so."

Rue tossed her hair to the side. "Yes, if you're totally dating Rush Limbaugh."

"C'mon girls," Darla declared. "We're getting nowhere fast!"

"Where do you want to shop at?" Brie asked.

"I really don't care," Darla answered. "I can find clothes to wear in any store."

"Like, I know what!" Rue grinned. "Each of us can totally go shopping on our own then we'll so meet back somewhere at a certain time."

"No way!" Darla piped up. "You'll get lost in here and we won't find you for a week."

Brie smiled. "That might be a good thing."

"Under normal circumstances, it would be awesome," Darla noted. "But we've got a job to do."

"Ok, since I'm the grown-up here, I'll compromise first." Brie placed a hand to her chest. "We can go to Forever 21 and then to Macy's. Is everybody happy?"

"Again, you're totally looking at me!" Rue turned around and walked while the other two followed.

After passing by several stores, Darla pointed. "There it is."

Rue shrieked. "I so love this place!" She took off, moving rather quickly.

"She's like a kid in a candy store." Brie entered last.

"Wow, it's pretty cool in here," Darla stated. "I've never shopped in a women's only store before, not even with my girlfriend."

Brie laughed. "Well, you are now with a different kind of girlfriend."

"I'm not sure if I'll ever get used to this," Darla remarked.

Brie huffed. "I don't want to."

Rue trotted up to them. "Look at all these way cool tops I found in the sales bin." She showed each one off. "Like, I just know they'll plunge down enough to show my cleavage—"

"And fall just shy of your bellybutton," Brie added. "Did you happen to see any blouses in there that are more traditional?"

"If you mean totally ugly then yeah, there's a whole bunch of them." Rue scrunched her face. "Like, nobody wants to look outdated."

"Do they have a shoe store in here?" Darla asked. "These heels I've got on are just too high."

"They don't, but we can majorly go to Nine West," Rue replied. "It's over by Victoria's Secret." Her face beamed. "We should totally go to both."

"Why?" Brie posed. "You don't wear bras or panties."

Rue smirked. "Like, you never know when I might get a major urge to wear one or both. Besides, my moms always told me to wear your best underwear in case you're ever in an accident. I want to look way good just in case I get a handsome paramedic saving my life."

"Oh, brother." Brie rolled her eyes.

"I so need some hot miniskirts to go with my way cool tops." Rue tossed her hair back. "Sales rack, here I come!" She rushed away.

"We should go and check out that sales bin," Brie said.

Darla nodded. "Don't forget, we need to buy female coats. I'm just glad I didn't have to wear my bomber jacket in here."

"That's why I prefer underground parking," Brie uttered. "We can don them and still be comfortable."

As they entered the clearance area, Rue was bent over the bin.

Brie leaned into Darla. "Oh, that's attractive." She cleared her throat. "Move over and let us look in here too."

Rue leaned back and pointed. "I totally tossed all the ugly items on the floor over there." She lifted up some newly-discovered items. "These skirts are to die for."

"How do you know what size you are?" Darla asked.

"Like, you need to totally grab what you like in various sizes then try them on to see what fits," Rue replied. "I'm so on my way to the dressing rooms now."

Brie and Darla finished with the sales bin and clearance racks. With clothes in hand, they walked back to try on their attire. As they approached, a blood-curdling scream echoed forth. A heavyset woman hurried toward them.

"Don't go in there," she shouted with arms flapping. "There's a man in the dressing room with a pair of lace panties on..." The sweat rolled down her forehead. "And I swear he was wearing make-up."

133

Her voice rasped. "I have to get the manager." The woman scuttled away.

"Oh, hell no!" Darla twitched.

"It couldn't be..." Brie's mouth dropped open.

They both darted toward the dressing rooms.

"Rue, where are you?" Darla roared.

"Show yourself!" Brie barked.

Only one had a locked door.

Darla pounded hard. "Open up!"

A male voice groused, "Like, what's your major malfunction?" He unlocked the door.

"What in blue blazes are you doing?" Brie shrieked. "Hurry and change back into Rue!"

"I'm trying," Russ yelped. "That woman totally scared the bejesus out of me and I couldn't concentrate!"

"Just do it!" Darla hollered. "They'll have you arrested."

"Like, I know!" Russ cringed. "I'm so trying!"

They heard voices as heavy footsteps headed their way.

"They're coming!" Brie gasped.

Two men turned the corner.

Darla covered her eyes while Brie looked down.

"Hello, ladies, we're sorry for the intrusion. I'm the store manager and this man is a security guard. Have any of you seen a man in the dressing area? It was reported that he was parading around in a pair of woman's underwear."

Brie and Darla turned their heads in Russ' direction.

"Like, it's only us three in here." Rue popped out her head. She held a garment up to cover her breasts. "Isn't that right, girls?"

"Uh-huh," Darla mumbled.

"Ah, yes," Brie murmured.

"If we totally see him, we'll let you know," Rue uttered.

The store manager examined the area. He opened the three remaining dressing room doors and turned around. "There's no sign of him anywhere."

"Maybe the woman was mistaken," the security guard said.

"Ladies, I'm sorry for the intrusion." The store manager tipped his head and they both walked away.

Darla leaned back and exhaled. "They're gone."

Brie slapped Rue on the arm. "What possessed you to pull a stunt like that?"

"Like, I wanted to feel the silk panties against my skin to see why some men are so turned on by them."

Brie stomped her foot. "You are such a whack job!"

"I totally—"

"Just save it!" Brie threw up her hand.

"Let's just try on these clothes to see what fits then beat feet," Darla stated.

Brie nodded and walked into a dressing room.

After making various choices, they collected their merchandise, brought it to the front of the store and checked out. Victoria's Secret was their next stop.

Before entering the store, Brie grabbed Rue's arm, stopping her dead. "Listen to me and listen well," she hissed through gritted teeth. "Do not, under any circumstances, change into a man unless it is a life-threatening situation. Do you hear me? And yes, I am threatening your life."

Rue pulled away, pouted and marched over to the see-through lingerie.

"Why're you looking at those?" Darla strolled over. "Don't you usually sleep in the nude?"

Rue nodded her head. "These are way cool though." She scanned the many styles.

Darla ran her fingers against a silk nightie. "Wow, this feels awesome."

135

"I would so wear this for that special someone." Rue touched it. "Like, I just had a thought—"

"Wow, I'm in awe!" Brie walked up.

Rue gave her the evil eye.

"Please, continue your thought," Brie stated. "I'm curious as to what will happen next."

Rue looked at Darla. "I could totally buy this and wear it as a girl when I have a boyfriend..." She grinned. "Or as a guy, I can so have my girlfriend wear it."

"Yuck! Gross," Brie remarked.

"Better yet, I can majorly date a guy and a girl at the same time, and switch when I'm in the mood or have a guy on one night, and a girl on another," Rue uttered. "Like, I could even have them both on the same night, at the same time. Wouldn't that be just wicked?"

Brie's face grimaced. "Yuck! Double gross."

"More of a double-cross!" Rue's mouth fell open. "They could totally fall for each other and leave me." She stopped, inhaled then giggled. "Like, that's so going to happen. I'm way too desirable." Her head tossed to the side. "What was I thinking?"

"Ah, you could be thinking about joining us back on Earth," Darla suggested.

"I doubt it," Brie countered. "She's landed on planet Smut."

"Rue, I thought you were getting a bra and a pair of panties for your paramedic," Darla mentioned. "Remember, we're on schedule."

She swooshed her hand in the air. "You can totally relax because I've decided we don't need to get a mani-pedi tonight."

"Oh, darn!" Darla smirked. "And I was so looking forward to getting them done."

"Me too." Brie snickered. "My twenty digits are in such dire straits."

Rue recoiled. "Like, you don't have to be so rude about it—"

"Oh, hell no!" Darla was wide-eyed as she pointed. "Isn't that Lydia and the Speaker of the House sitting over at that table outside the coffee shop?"

Brie edged up. "Yes, it is."

Rue leaned in. "They're totally having a powwow—"

"And it looks quite heated," Brie added.

"Like, one of you should majorly go over and eavesdrop," Rue uttered. "Lydia knows what I look like so I can't."

"I can't either," Darla stated. "I woke up next to her as a woman. She might've seen me."

"Lydia way told me she couldn't remember any of it," Rue remarked.

Brie laughed. "Chalk that one up to liquor overload!"

"Like, that seemed to be the running theme of the evening," Rue quipped.

"So, am I doing this?" Darla asked.

"I totally think Brie should do it," Rue replied.

"Why should I?" She squawked. "I especially hate people, and certainly do not want to hear about their pathetic lives."

"You're so the least noticeable amongst us," Rue responded. "With Darla's flaming-red, wavy hair and my bouncing blonde curls and beauty, we'd totally stick out like sore thumbs."

"And, what am I, a potted plant?" Brie huffed.

"You totally wanted to go the all-natural route." Rue gestured. "Plant your pot in the seat next to them and act way natural."

Brie sneered. "Are you kidding me?"

"Like, you're a plain Jane with mousy, brown hair and bland features," Rue retorted. "So, with no outstanding presence, you'd be the likely choice."

Darla gasped. "Oh, no she didn't."

"Yes, the bitch did!" Brie snarled.

137

"I'm just saying it'll be way easier for you to blend in." Rue tilted her head. "And I didn't mean for it to sound mean; I'm so not like that."

"You could have fooled me," Brie hissed.

"Just get a cup of coffee, sit close to them, and listen," Darla suggested. "It'll be easy-peasy."

"Fine," Brie blurted out. "I'll be right back."

"Like, wait!"

"What?" Brie stopped.

"Totally take my micro recorder and way tape what you hear," Rue urged.

Darla chuckled. "You do carry that everywhere, don't you?"

"I've so told you before, it's like my Visa..." Rue grinned. "I never leave home without it."

Brie sneered. "I thought that was your diaphragm."

Rue pointed. "Like, go!"

Brie turned and left. She bought a coffee along with a newspaper and sat down near Lydia and Logan. Several minutes later, she got up and walked back over to the girls.

"Listen to this!" She pushed a button.

"Harvey was my mole; keeping an eye on those fools," Logan stated. "Unfortunately, he got all greedy and tried to extort a better standing for himself; to leverage his position as my right-hand man. Well, let's just say it backfired on him. I had Arvin level him out."

"What if you cannot control the President?" Lydia asked.

"Then I will discredit him," Logan answered. "A few doses should turn him into a babbling fool. He'll be impeached. When VP Graves gets put in his place, I'll deal the underage girls' card right into the hands of the media. With that pig out of the way, I'm next in line. How does becoming my First Lady sound to you?"

Lydia exhaled. "It sounds heavenly!"

"I'm not stopping there," Logan continued. "I'll serve the world to you on a silver platter. Once I take office, I'll use the formula on

138

the United Nations. That should keep most countries at bay, and if not, I will use my formula during meetings with each world leader. They will be on my side in no time," he said. "Oh, look at the time! Baby, I've got to get to a meeting."

Brie stopped the recording. "Can you believe this guy?"

"I believe he's a psychopath," Darla replied.

"More like a megalomaniac," Brie countered. "We have to stop him."

"Like, we so have to stop Lydia from going to work tomorrow," Rue insisted. "She's the one way perfecting their secret formula."

"Well, we'll just use our secret formula on her," Brie remarked.

"What's that?" Darla asked.

"It's a little something I like to call—alcohol." Brie smiled. "We order the drinks for the night, making them doubles and even triples. Once she gets slopped up, it'll all taste the same."

Rue giggled. "Mission: Chivas Regal!"

When the three of them finished laughing, they headed toward Nine West and walked into the store.

"Ooh, look at all these shoes." Rue beamed. "Aren't they totally delicious?"

Brie looked at Darla. "She's found her mother-ship."

A salesman walked up. "Hi, my name is Paul. Can I help you find anything? Maybe take your shoe size?"

Rue pointed and latched onto his sturdy bicep. "Like, I'll take everything on the left side of the wall in a size six, please."

"You must be hallucinating!" Brie snickered. "Your foot is at least a size seven and a half; if not an eight!"

Rue twirled around and stuck out her tongue. With a slow turn of her head, a sexy smile was flashed at the salesman. "So, what size do you totally think I am?" She hung off his arm.

"Well, um..." He looked down at her feet. "I, ah..." The guy cleared his throat. "I'd guesstimate you're a size seven." His head stayed down.

Rue nuzzled against him. "Like, you're probably right."

139

The salesman smiled and looked into her eyes. "I can measure your feet then we'll know the true size."

Her eyes gleamed. "You're way sweet."

His shoulders puffed. "Why don't you come over here and I'll have you sit down?"

Rue nodded. "Like, totally."

The salesman guided her to the shoe bench. She eased off his arm and sat down. He knelt, reached over and grabbed a metal object. "Here, put your foot on this."

Rue placed it onto the device.

The salesman moved a couple of knobs around then looked at her. "I was right! You're a perfect size seven."

Brie leaned into Darla. "Did he have to say the word—perfect?"

"I know," she replied. "We'll never, and I mean, ever hear the end of that."

The salesman grinned. "I'll be right back." Off he went.

"Rue, don't run him ragged," Brie stated. "We need shoes too."

"Why don't you totally go over to that rack and get a pair of Birkenstocks." She swished her hand. "You so say you're the all-natural type; they're way lesbian chic, and that would be such an easy look for you to pull off."

Brie gritted her teeth.

The salesman came back with his arms full of boxes and put them down on the floor. He looked over at Brie and Darla. "I'll help you two in a few minutes."

"No, we can help ourselves," Brie grunted. "C'mon, Darla." She yanked her away by the arm.

The salesman opened box after box to fit Rue with an assortment of heels, flats and sandals. When finally done, he brought them to the register. Rue walked over to Brie and Darla.

"Like, I'm so worn out."

"So is my patience," Brie added.

140

"These are all that we've picked so far." Darla pointed to three pairs of flats.

"Are you totally for real?" Rue clamored.

"It's not as if we had a boy-toy massaging our feet while putting shoes on them," Brie retorted.

Rue pursed her lips. "Like, he just tickled them for a moment."

"Oh, I'm sorry for that foot faux pas." Brie placed a hand against her chest. "Tickling, massaging, rubbing, stroking; it's all the same when you're flirting with a guy."

"Like, whatever!" Rue tossed her hair to the side. "He's totally giving me a store discount for being so nice to him."

"I'm shocked he didn't ask you out on a date," Brie remarked.

Rue snickered. "He so asked me out."

Brie threw her hands into the air. "Well, that shock wore off fast."

"He's way giving you girls a discount too!" Rue uttered.

Brie turned. "What?"

Darla chimed in. "She said—"

"I heard her!" A slight smile eased over Brie's lips. "We need to buy some shoes."

Rue grabbed a pair of heels. "Here, totally take these." She handed them over. "Like, climb off your high horse and climb onto these stilettos."

Darla laughed. "There's no way she'll be able to walk in those."

Brie snatched them out of Rue's hands. "Just watch me!"

"Oh, I wouldn't miss this for anything," Darla stated.

Brie put on the heels and clod-hopped around; her arms outstretched, flailing for balance.

"Like, totally slow down, Godzilla!" Rue razzed her. "You're so not attacking Tokyo—"

"Or doing battle with King Kong," Darla added.

Brie dropped to her knees. "I hate these things, along with the both of you"

141

Darla and Rue grabbed her by the arms and helped her up.

"Like, maybe you should totally go with a way lower heel."

"You think?" Brie wiped off her knees.

"I definitely think." Darla strapped on a pair of heels and strolled effortlessly around. "Wow, this is a synch!"

Brie glared at her.

After searching for the perfect footwear, the girls purchased their items and left the store.

Darla looked at Rue. "The salesman really liked you."

"They all like her," Brie quipped. "She's blonde and beautiful with a hot body. Men can't help themselves from falling all over her. It's hard-wired in their brains. My mother's neighbor was of that species. She told me that all the neighborhood men would stare at her and make comments to each other, much to the chagrin of their wives. My mother and the other women called it the Bimbo Blitz."

"I totally altered this way," Rue uttered. "Like, it's not my fault that my hormones made me so gorgeous!"

"Just drop it," Brie requested. "One day, we might need to enact the Bimbo Blitz, but today isn't that day."

Darla snapped her fingers. "Ladies, time's a ticking."

"There's Macy's!" Brie pointed. "Let's go inside and end this escapade."

With heads nodding, all three entered the store.

Rue trotted toward the makeup counter. She walked around it and saw Darla at the perfume display. After turning to the side, she noticed Brie at the jewelry receptacle. They meandered around the various shelves and purchased items as they went along. When finished, the three met and decided to go to the women's bathroom to get ready. Once inside, they placed their bags on the counter and opened them.

"Like, I picked up some eye shadow, liner, mascara, blush, lipstick and face-cleansing pads." Each was pulled out of the shopping bag.

142

"I bought several different perfumes," Darla commented. "They all smelled so good, it was hard to get just one."

"Here!" Brie handed Rue a small velvet box. "Since you're ears are pierced, I thought you might like these."

"Like, oh my God!" Her eyes welled up as she opened the item.

"Whoa, diamond studs!" Darla leaned in. "Someone is apologizing."

With tears flowing down her face, Rue grabbed Brie and hugged her.

Darla smiled.

"There, there..." Brie rubbed Rue's back. "You didn't need to get that emotional. For goodness sakes, they're only earrings. You're acting like I bought you a country house in the Hamptons."

She released her embrace as a slight giggle replaced the sniveling. "I'm so sorry about the shoe store." Rue inhaled. "Like, I just wanted some help with the shoes."

"And maybe a little discount," Darla added.

Rue sniffled. "A major one."

"Well, now you need to be careful." Brie cautioned. "A guy will read much more into it than is really there. You know as guys, we've all been down that road."

"Some of us faster than others," Darla remarked.

"Just be aware of the power you now wield over men," Brie imparted. "Some women will use that allure to get what they want. There's even some who'll coyly flirt with a guy to get their own boyfriend jealous; not realizing that he'll get aggravated and battle to save face. That's what we call low self-esteem."

"If men and women could swap genders for just one day they'd know how the opposite sex thinks and feels, and there'd never be another argument between them, except maybe over money," Darla stated. "We're quite fortunate that our alter egos give us the chance to see both sides of the coin."

"Like, that way we can so check ourselves before we wreck ourselves," Rue quipped.

"Exactly!" Darla agreed.

Brie rubbed the outside of Rue's upper arms. "You need to use your new power for good and not evil, unless of course we're taking down a culprit or two. Then release the Kraken!"

Rue giggled while nodding with approval.

Brie dropped her hands, grabbed a narrow box and handed it to Darla. "Here, I bought you a little something too."

"Thanks!" Her eyes widened while opening it. "Wow, a gold necklace. I've wanted one of these." She put it on. "Cool, it's long enough so I can wear it as a guy too!"

"If you haven't noticed, it matches your gold bracelet," Brie mentioned.

"I did!" Darla beamed. "I'm also noticing there's a warm heart in your cold exterior after all."

"Don't spread it around. I've a reputation to uphold." Brie cracked a half-smile. "Besides, I needed a lady's timepiece anyways, so I figured why not make myself look good in the process." She put the watch around her wrist. "Once in a while, even I need a slight ego boost to keep me on my game."

Darla chuckled. "What time is it?"

Brie finished tightening the watch. "Close to 9:00pm."

"Let's totally get a move on, chicks!" Rue grabbed her shopping bags. She ran into a stall and locked it.

"Well, Darla, I guess we've got to share the other."

"It'll just take me a second to dress," Rue called out.

"That's because there's not much to put on," Brie commented. "But, then again, there's not that much to cover."

"You're so right," Rue uttered. "I've got such an itty bitty waistline."

"Please, your hips and breasts well make up the difference," Brie bellowed.

"Like, whatever!" Rue opened the stall door. She walked up to the sink counter, opened the cleansing pads and began wiping her face.

144

"Darla, go into the other one," Brie barked. "I cannot get ready with your big rear in my way."

Darla huffed then left the stall. She looked at Rue. "Wow, that outfit is hot!"

She tossed her hair to the side. "I majorly wanted a much smaller size, but there weren't any."

"Really?" Darla declared. "Just one good sneeze and you'd be arrested for indecent exposure."

Rue giggled, turning toward the mirror. "I've got to so beat my mug."

"You should leave it alone and let it heal," Brie yelled.

"Ignore her," Darla stated. "What does it mean?"

"It so means to put on your make-up." Rue applied some eye shadow. "Like, I way saw the phrase in a fashion magazine."

"I'll have to remember that one," Darla noted. "I guess there's some new slang that needs to be learned if I want to understand female conversations."

"Totally!" Rue expressed. "It's a whole new world." She thickened her lashes with mascara. "I so liked being a guy, but I so love being a girl."

"Shouldn't you two be getting ready instead of cackling?" Brie croaked from inside the stall. "There you go, Darla. You've now got another phrase to add to your feminine repertoire."

Rue brushed the blush along her cheekbones. "Like, what about clamming up?"

Darla snickered. "I see the niceties from earlier have left the room."

"And so will your head if you don't get into the stall and dress," Brie snarled.

"I just need my zipper done up," Darla mentioned. "I didn't want to bother you while you were putting on your girdle."

"They are called Spanx," Brie snapped. "It's supposed to give one a shapelier figure."

Rue tossed her lipstick into a small clutch. "Like, I hope you're putting on two; maybe even a third."

145

"So, what are you trying to say?" Brie squawked.

"That you totally need some smaller shoulders, bigger boobs and fuller hips," Rue responded.

"Ouch!" Darla belted out.

"Well, I guess I'll have to make an appointment with Dr. Frankenstein and have him shave down my mammoth shoulders," Brie remarked. "Then he can take the excess off the floor and shove them into my nonexistent hips while pumping industrial-grade silicone in my chest to make them a forty-four double D. That way, I can wiggle and jiggle like a floozy."

"Like, now you're getting the gist," Rue uttered.

Brie sneered. "Wow, the day I take body image recommendations from Glinda the Good Wench of the North, is the day I fly south on a broomstick!"

"Totally down to Antarctica, one hopes," Rue reacted.

Brie exited the stall. "You mean to tell me that you got yourself together and ridiculed me at the same time?" She smirked. "I thought being blonde and all, you wouldn't be able to do two things at once."

Rue scanned her outfit. "I so need to say one word—humdrum."

Brie put a hand to her hip. "Well, I've got a couple of them." She pointed. "Your make-up is way too heavy. That skirt is way too short and your breasts are popping out with your muffin top. Not to mention you smell like a gutter tramp, and those heels make you look like one. Not even a crack whore would be caught dead looking that trashy."

Darla chuckled. "Just a couple of words, huh?"

Brie looked at her watch. "I could muster up a few more paragraphs, but I'm sure she got the gist. Anyhow, a lady of flawless style, elegant decorum and greater taste should keep her conversation to a minimum."

"Like, you're at the maximum words with that grody taste and average decorum; plus your flawed style of a middle-aged housewife attending a church fundraiser bores me," Rue uttered. "This look is way sexier, my make-up is incredible, and this dress fits as snug as a bug in a rug."

146

"Sure, a throw rug," Brie quipped.

Darla snickered. "When you two are finished with this montage to Vogue, I'd like to have my make-up done. Wait a minute! I'd like my mug beaten."

Brie sneered. "Oh, it will be, and by the back of my hand."

"Totally ignore her." Rue picked up a makeup brush. "Like, I've already picked out colors that will accentuate your outfit."

"Well, the ones you chose don't accentuate yours," Brie countered. "If anything, it took away from it, and believe me you don't need any more taken away."

"Enough!" Darla blurted out. "I'm not listening to this bickering all night. You got me?"

Both girls nodded in silence.

"Good!" Darla looked to Rue. "I'm ready for my mug-beating." She flung her finger out and pointed at Brie. "Not a word."

All was quiet.

Rue looked toward Brie as she applied the different colors on Darla's face. "Like, are you going to wear some makeup?"

"Of course not," she replied. "I'm naturally beautiful."

"So is an alligator's rectum, but I'd still spit shine it before making it into a purse or a pair of shoes."

Darla laughed.

"Like, I'm joking!" Rue waved the blush brush at her. "I'll so make you look less hard and rough."

Brie cocked her head. "You should have become a comedienne instead of being a detective. You're much better at it."

"Ha...ha...ha!" Rue finished fluffing up Darla's hair. "You're totally done."

"That doesn't look half bad." Brie rushed to the counter and ran a cleansing pad over her face. "You can put on a little, but if you make me look awful, I will be livid."

"Like, your parents already took care of that, so it can only get better from here."

147

"Again, with the funny." Brie glared at her. "Just don't screw it up, and remember, I said just a tad."

Darla peered in the mirror. "Wow, I look really good! Thank you." She turned and put her cheek against Rue's.

"You're so welcome." Rue picked up the mascara. "Now the real work totally begins."

After her makeup was applied, Brie stood up and looked into the mirror. With widened eyes, she gasped. "I am in utter shock."

"That you look good?" Darla asked.

"No, that she actually listened to me," Brie retorted.

"Are we done?" Darla was ready to go.

"It so looks it!" Rue gathered everything together and put it into the shopping bags. The others followed suit.

When finished, they all took one last look at themselves.

Rue smiled at her work. "Darla, you're majorly beautiful; I'm incredibly stunning, and Brie looks somewhat good."

A thunderous voice echoed from the loud speakers. "Macy's is now closing. Please, bring your items to purchase then exit out the first level entranceway."

"We're on the third floor," Brie remarked. "I hope they don't lock us in."

Darla huffed. "We've got to get cracking."

"Just not our faces," Rue uttered. "Like, they need to stay totally smooth all night!"

They laughed, picked up their bags and dashed out the door.

Chapter 10

In the distance, the exquisite Alabaster Hotel rose along the scenic skyline of Washington, DC. Built in 1914, each room featured nouveau designs of the art deco period. With valet parking and fine dining, they catered to the affluent members of society.

"This place is beautiful!" Brie pulled the car up to the curb.

"There's Lydia standing in the lobby." Darla pointed.

Rue waved from the backseat. "Remember girls, she's a totally learned woman so don't act like a couple of fools."

"Who do you think we are, Abbott and Costello?" Brie sneered.

Rue recoiled. "Who?"

"Never mind," Brie replied.

"Like, whatever!"

The backdoor opened and Lydia got in.

Rue piped up. "Let me totally introduce you to my girlfriends."

Lydia nodded. "Sure."

Brie and Darla turned around.

Lydia gasped. "Your hair is the most stunning red that I have ever seen."

"Thanks!" Her hand stroked the waves. "It's my natural hair color. And my name's Darla, by the way."

"You are so fortunate," Lydia stated. "Women in my country spend top dollar to get that color done to their hair."

Rue gestured. "Like, the girl driving is Brie."

149

"Hello, I am Lydia. Which I am sure you both figured out by now."

Brie looked in the rearview mirror. "Hello." She shifted then drove off.

"So Lydia, how're you doing?" Rue asked.

"I will be fine once I get a drink in me."

"Or two," Darla added.

"Better yet, three," Brie chimed in.

"My girlfriends mean we're so going to have a majorly good time," Rue uttered.

"Good," Lydia said. "I need a night of fun."

Brie snickered. "That you shall have."

"Rue, your dress is so chic," Lydia commented. "I just love the plunging neckline."

"It shows off her ample cleavage," Darla added.

Rue giggled. "And so don't forget my ravaging bod."

"Just be careful," Lydia advised. The guys will want to ravage it. Although, I would say, ravage away."

Brie looked at Darla and rolled her eyes. "Ah, I hate to break up this love-fest, but we're here."

"Wow, look at all the people standing in line!" Darla exclaimed. "It's going to take hours to get inside."

As a guy walked up to their car, Brie put the window down.

"Would you lovely ladies like me to valet park your car?"

Rue opened the window and arched her back. "Like, how much will it cost?" she asked, heaving out her bosom.

As his eyes expanded, he grinned. "It's free to you, beautiful."

"Free is way too expensive." Rue pouted. "Could you so wash our car, too?"

"I'm sorry," he responded. "We don't provide that service, but if we did I'd have definitely done it for you."

"I guess we'll have to totally settle for free." Rue opened her door.

The valet grabbed her hand and escorted her to the curb. The other girls got out of the car and met up with her.

"Must you flirt with every man you see?" Brie asked. "Maybe one of us would have wanted him."

"Like who, you?" Rue answered. "Are you seriously suggesting that he'd even look at you with me here?" Her hand fluttered. "Why would he so want a sip of draft beer when he could be uncorking a bottle of Dom Perignon?"

Brie reached her clawed hand out.

"That's not on our agenda tonight." Darla grabbed Brie's arm. "Remember our mission is to get soused and pick up some men."

"That is my mission," Lydia stated.

A stocky man came up to them. "Hi ladies, follow me." He led them around the red velvet rope and up to the front door. "Hot women always bump the line and get in for free."

After they all entered the club, Lydia and Rue sashayed up to the bar as Brie and Darla followed.

"What can I get you babes to drink?" the bartender asked.

"What is your name?" Lydia asked in return.

"I'm Jacob," he replied, his blue eyes radiating.

"I will take one of you on the rocks." Lydia smiled.

He grinned. "I like the sand better."

"Especially, if it is wet," Lydia added.

Brie barged in. "Speaking of wet, my whistle needs to be."

"I've got this," Darla chimed in. "Could I please order three Diet Pepsi's and a Chivas Regal on the rocks?"

Brie leaned against the bar. "Bartender..." She lowered her voice. "Would you make that Chivas Regal a double?"

He nodded.

"Why are you girls not drinking?" Lydia asked.

151

"I so don't drink, and they always start out with a soda before totally hitting the hard stuff." Rue turned aside to whisper. "Like, they're both major lightweights when it comes to alcohol."

Lydia winked. "I got it."

The bartender brought them their drinks.

"Thank you, handsome." Lydia picked up the glass. She gulped down the contents, placed it on the bar and ordered another. "It tastes so smooth."

"Like, you go, girl!" Rue bubbled.

Brie leaned into Darla. "A couple more and we'll be in bed quite early tonight."

"Then let's get this job done."

Lydia edged in holding another cocktail. "Do you have boyfriends?"

Brie and Darla look at each other.

"I met Rue's last night at a bar, but for some reason he felt under the weather—"

"Did you find him handsome?" Brie interjected.

"Yes, I did." Lydia squinted. "Your features are very similar to his. Are you related?'

"As a matter of fact we are," she replied. "He's my twin brother."

Lydia nudged Rue with her elbow. "I see you are keeping it in the family."

Brie winked at Darla. "I heard you met quite a fella last night."

"Yes, I did." Lydia smiled. "He was so much fun." She swilled back her drink. "I hope he calls me."

"Oh, I'm sure he will," Brie crowed. "If he's half the man I think he is."

"I so love this song!" Rue swayed back and forth as the music blasted its hypnotic beat. "Like, let's go dance."

"Not even close," Darla countered.

Brie shook her head. "It's not my cup of tea."

152

"Like, we are so doing this." Rue and Lydia latched onto the girls' arms and dragged them onto the dance floor.

"I don't know how to dance," Darla roared over the pulsating music.

"Just jiggle your feet and totally wiggle your hips like me," Rue shouted while wildly gyrating.

"If I danced like that I'd break my hip," Brie bellowed.

"It is all about moving to the beat of the music," Lydia yelled, swiveling her derriere.

After dancing along to several songs, they walked off the dance floor.

"I'm thirsty," Darla remarked.

"Yes, quite parched," Brie added. "Plus, it's so loud in here I can't hear myself think."

As they headed toward the bar, the music faded in the distance.

"That's way better..." Rue slung her hair to the side. "Sounding like a carnival barker is so not my thing."

"I know what you mean," Lydia stated. "With such deafening music, it is difficult to appear as a lady when you have to shout like a gentleman."

"Like, so true," Rue quipped.

They stood at the bar in a tight circle.

"I'll get this round," Brie spoke up. "Does everybody want the same?"

All three nodded.

"You girls are still drinking soda?" Lydia asked.

"Brie and I have quite the hangovers from too many drinks last night that we're letting our systems drain," Darla answered. "I'm sure my liver is still soaked."

"I understand," Lydia noted. "I have been there a couple of times myself."

"It feels so good going down, but not so much coming up," Darla commented.

"Here are your drinks." Brie handed them out.

"I will get the next round," Lydia said.

"Way cool!" Rue grabbed Lydia's arm. "Like, let's go to the ladies room so we can powder our noses."

Darla leaned into Brie. "What does that mean?"

"That's probably one of the phrases we need to know," she replied. "Just follow what they're doing and learn."

They walked to the far left corner of the building.

"Why is there always a line at the ladies bathroom?" Lydia asked. "No matter the different countries I have been to, there is always a long wait."

"I guess it's totally an international problem," Rue responded.

"Instead of fixing immigration, they should resolve this issue," Lydia stated. "Imagine the votes they would get from the women."

"Like amen, sister," Rue quipped.

Ten minutes later, they were finally admitted into the bathroom. As all four walked up to the mirror, Rue looked at her reflection and grimaced.

"Grody, why didn't anybody tell me I looked this heinous?"

Brie sneered. "I figured it was a given."

"I think you look beautiful," Darla commented.

Rue grabbed some items out of her clutch and freshened her face.

"I also need a complete overhaul." Lydia reached into her purse.

Brie removed the exact items from her handbag. She picked up each one and mimicked the application process. Darla watched on.

Rue stepped back and looked at herself. "Like, mirror, mirror, on the wall, who is the most stunning of them all?"

She was shoved aside. "My pet, my pet, please do not fret, I have to warn of a powerful threat. You see for me, I must decree, there is another more stunning than thee, so wallow in your misery and meet the lovely girl named Brie!"

Rue added. "Who so hangs from the branch of a tree—"

154

"And feeds on the bottom of the sea." Darla finished it.

Lydia laughed.

"Everybody thinks they're a comedian," Brie bellowed.

"You totally mean comedienne," Rue countered.

"In response, I need to quote an absolute dingbat..." Brie snickered. "Whatever!"

Rue smirked. "Like, whatever!"

Lydia's cell phone rang. She fumbled around in her purse to retrieve it. "Hello?" She put it on speaker.

"Hi, baby, it's Logan."

"Hello, honey!" She fluffed her hair.

"I know it's late, but do you want to come over? I've got a bottle of champagne chilling and we can have a glass before going to bed. You know that makes me—"

"Logan..." She cut him off. "I will not be able to tonight."

"Why?" he asked. "We could get up early and have breakfast together then I'll drive you to work. Wouldn't that be nice on your first day?"

"Yes, but I am out with a friend," she replied. "The one I met yesterday at the Back Alley Bar.

"Oh, right...the blonde with all the hair."

"Yes, her name is Rue Munroe."

"Well, you shouldn't stay out too late." He stressed. "You're starting the new position early in the morning."

"Yes, I am quite aware of the situation."

"You haven't said anything about Prescott Chemicals or that you're working on the formula?"

"Of course not!" Lydia lied. She looked at Rue and smiled. "Hold for a moment. I want to find a less congested area." All four walked out of the bathroom, bypassed the men's room and clustered together in a tranquil corner.

155

"Oh, baby, I wish you were coming over," Logan whined. "I've been privy to something of inherent importance and need to share it with you before I explode."

"Tell me now," she said. "What has got my man so hot and bothered?"

"No, your friend is with you," Logan replied. "I don't want any liabilities this late in the game."

"She went to the ladies' room," Lydia declared. "I will forewarn you when she appears."

Logan exhaled. "I'm still nervous that someone might overhear us."

"Honey, what if I tell you what I am wearing under my very tight and very short mini-dress? Would it give you the incentive to talk?"

"Oh, it most certainly would."

Lydia inhaled. "I have nothing on." She exhaled. "How do you feel now?"

"Much, much better," Logan popped off. "I'm ready to confess."

"I am listening." Lydia purred.

"My friend, Thurston Young, who's the President pro Tempore of the Senate, is playing ball with us." Logan confided. "He has locked in the help of Senator Davis Palmer of Virginia with some campaign promises. Supposedly, this guy has a couple of judges in his pocket. They will make sure any and all evidence that is brought in gets the magic touch. Abracadabra and poof!"

Brie, Darla and Rue stared at one another with eyes wide open.

"You seem to be tying up all the loose ends," Lydia stated.

"In a big, fat bow!" Logan boasted. "And that's not even the best part. Senator Palmer is married to Vivienne Vassar, daughter of billionaire Winston Vassar. Not only does her family have exhaustive connections, and the money to stabilize them, she's also a brilliant lawyer. This woman went to Stanford for her masters then on to Harvard, which is her father's alma mater, for her law degree where she placed in the top percentile."

"I am quite impressed."

156

"What's impressive is how she got a mistrial verdict for Vince Endicott last year for the attempted assassination of the President and the slayings of the driver and two bodyguards. Vivienne exposed a cover up and along with forged documents, manipulated evidence and hidden agendas that corrupt officers and their commanding officials tried to keep sealed."

"Why do you need her?"

"She'll be my get-out-of-jail-free card just in case one of the bungling idiots who're helping me get to the presidency, well, bungle it up," Logan answered. "You know one of those imbeciles will throw me under the bus if given a deal from the prosecution. I'm just saving my ass ahead of time."

"What makes you so sure she will help you?"

"Let's just say her father has an indiscretion that needs to be kept under wraps, under the covers if you know what I mean—"

"My friend has departed the ladies room and is on her way back," Lydia whispered. "I will talk to you tomorrow. Goodbye." She hung up.

"Let's totally leave this area." Rue's face scrunched. "It smells so grody this close to the men's room."

They turned and walked out of the alcove.

Lydia pointed. "We should sit down on those sofas over there."

"Sounds good to me!" Darla agreed. "My hooves are killing me."

"Like, a lady should never admit that her feet hurt," Rue declared.

Brie huffed. "Who cares about etiquette when your feet are aching?"

After they traipsed over and sat down, smiles came over their sullen faces.

"This sofa is so plush that I sank right in." Brie sighed.

"That totally happens to heavier girls." Rue crossed her legs.

Brie scoffed. "I see the comedienne is back."

Rue turned away and leaned into Lydia. "Like, look at that guy near the end of the bar in the black leather jacket." Her head motioned. "He's so smiling at you."

157

"What about Logan?" Darla asked. "You're not going to do something behind his back, are you?"

"Behind the back, in front of him or to his sides..." Brie remarked. "That conniving jerk has to go." She stuck out her thumb.

"I have been contemplating this very issue." Lydia nodded. "Logan has business dealings with some unscrupulous men and I do not want any part of it," she said. "I will end my relationship tomorrow."

Rue faced her. "Sweetie, the best way to get over an old flame is to just blow it out," she uttered. "Then you totally ignite a new one who's scorching hot and blazing with heat."

Lydia shrugged. "Should I flirt with him?"

"Why not?" Brie replied. "You could add another to your roster."

"What does that mean?" Lydia asked.

Rue glared at Brie. "Like, it's sort of a date book..." She fidgeted with her fingers. "You've so got another man to totally go out with."

Lydia smiled. "My mother always said that a girl can never have too many admirers or too much money."

Brie leaned into Darla. "I guess the apple doesn't fall far from the family tree."

She whispered back. "That motto should be tramp-stamped on her chest."

Lydia looked around. "There is a smorgasbord of men here. All of us should be able to add a man to our roster. Am I right?"

Brie and Darla sat with their hands crossed.

"Like, here comes that guy, and he's bringing a friend." Rue took out her compact.

"Let the games begin," Brie mumbled.

"Hi, my name is Kurt, and this here is my buddy, Greg. Would you and your blonde friend care to dance?"

"We would love to," Lydia replied. She snatched Rue's hand and yanked her off the sofa. They handed their purses to Brie and Darla.

Kurt took Lydia's hand and they walked off.

Rue grabbed Greg's arm and headed toward the dance floor.

"Can you believe that Lydia allowed us to hear that information?" Darla asked.

"She probably figured since we don't know her that well that we'd have no idea what they were talking about or possibly didn't care," Brie replied. "She also put it on speaker to leave her hands free so she could mess with her hair."

"Either way, she helped us out big time." Darla chuckled.

Brie grinned. "Quite true!"

Two men came up to them.

"Would you care to dance with us?" one of them asked.

"No, I wouldn't," Brie responded. She grabbed Darla's hand. "This is my significant other."

The guys stood back, looked at each other and scooted away.

"And that's how you do that!" Brie snapped her fingers.

A waiter was nearby.

"Sir," Darla yelled, waving her hand.

He came over.

"Would you get us some drinks?" she asked.

"Certainly," he replied. "What's your poison?"

"I'll take three non-poisonous Diet Pepsi's and a Chivas Regal on the rocks; a double, please."

"Make it a triple," Brie added. "And tell the bartender to render it lethal!"

"I most certainly will." The waiter walked away.

"A job worth doing well is a job well done," Brie declared.

Darla put her hand to her mouth and laughed out loud.

"If you really want to laugh, look at them on the dance floor." Brie pointed. "Rue is throwing her hips around like a stripper and Lydia is dirty dancing all up and down that guy."

As they looked on, two women entered the dance floor and went up to Rue and Lydia. Soon, a screaming match ensued, but was quickly broken up.

Darla leaned in. "What do you think happened?"

"Those two girls were most likely hit on by those guys, and didn't want Lydia and Rue muscling in on their property," Brie replied. "Girls get territorial real quick when there's a man shortage, especially when they're handsome."

The waiter came up and placed their drinks on the table.

"Ooh..." Darla scrunched her face. "I can smell the toxic cocktail from here."

The waited dipped his head.

Brie reached into Lydia's purse and retrieved her wallet. She pulled out a credit card, gave it to him then looked at Darla. "Well, she did say the next round was on her."

The waiter ran the plastic through a device then passed it back with a receipt.

"Thank you..." Brie pulled some money out of Lydia's wallet and handed it to him. "This is for you," she said. "Would you check back with us soon?"

"I will," he replied, looking at the cash. "I definitely will." The waiter turned around and trotted away.

"Did you just hand him a fifty?" Darla asked.

Brie smiled. "Lydia is such a big tipper."

Once again, they broke out in laughter.

Rue and Lydia walked up and sat down. Both looked quite miserable.

"Did your foursome fall through?" Brie snickered.

"Like, can you believe those guys had girlfriends?" Rue scoffed. "They totally went off on Lydia and I then turned on their boyfriends so we skedaddled."

160

"Well, I ordered some drinks for us," Brie stated.

"I was supposed to buy this round," Lydia declared.

Brie slurped her soda through a straw. "You did!"

Lydia picked up her Chivas Regal. "What do you girls do for a living?"

"Like, we're hookers," Rue blurted out.

Soda shot out of Brie's mouth as Lydia gasped.

"Tell her you're joking," Darla ordered.

Rue tossed back her hair. "I'm totally teasing."

"What are your actual occupations?" Lydia swilled her drink.

"Like, I'm a hairstylist and they're flight attendants." Rue giggled. "One could so argue they're air hookers."

Brie scowled. "Oh, you and I will be arguing—"

"Lydia, what will be your position at Prescott Chemicals?" Darla chimed in.

"I am a physicist," she replied. "I was hired to assist another man with a formulation. I am not supposed to let anybody know about what I will be working on. But you are now my friends so I will tell you."

"Way cool!" Rue quipped. "I'm so curious about what you do." She prodded her on. "It must be wickedly fascinating."

Lydia smiled. "I am working on a classified formula for a green pesticide presently referred to as TB4711."

"That would be great for the environment," Brie stated.

"It will be once I work on it." Lydia slurped her drink.

"Do you know how to fix it?" Darla probed.

"It is just a matter of getting the inert ratio metered to a refined calculation." Lydia took another swig.

"I'm totally clueless as to what that means." Rue shrugged.

Lydia laughed. "It must have been the alcohol talking."

"I thought maybe you had lapsed into French," Brie remarked.

"A basic explanation would do me just fine," Darla said.

161

Lydia gulped down the rest of her drink and put the glass down. "The man that I will be assisting has already computed the existing equations that were developed. I will take them and adjust the formulation to its specified cohesive degree while I fraction out the phlegmatic theorem to achieve exponential congruency with equilateral integration."

"That was much better!" Brie leaned against Darla. "The broad is blotto."

A man approached them. "Could I entice one of you beautiful ladies to dance with me?"

"I will!" Lydia hopped up, grabbed his arm, and pulled him away.

"Holy moly!" Darla shook her head.

Brie sneered. "There's nothing holy there."

"Like, I think she's groovy," Rue uttered.

"That's hardly shocking," Brie declared. "As Russ, you always chased after the trashy ones."

Rue glared, sipping her soda.

"Well, call her what you may," Darla stated. "At least she's getting liquored up and loose with the lips."

Brie snickered. "Speak of the devil."

Lydia tottered up, laughing to herself. "That was quite fun." She swayed, slurring the words. "He is really hot."

Rue moved over and patted the sofa. "Sweetie, sit down here."

"Where's the hot man?" Darla looked around.

Lydia plopped down. "He is getting us some drinks from the bar." Her words garbled together. "I ordered each of you a soda, but if you want something stronger to drink, I will pay for them."

Brie looked at her watch. "No, the club will be closing soon, and I'm quite tired."

"Me too," Darla added. "I need to throw myself back in the sack and catch me some more Z's."

Lydia's head teetered. "Oh, I invited him back to my hotel room for a nightcap and he agreed." She burst forth with laughter.

"What's so funny?" Darla shrugged.

As her glee subsided, Lydia grinned. "He does not know that I am the nightcap."

Rue smirked. "Like, no way!"

"The nightcap is coming," Brie beckoned.

Lydia sat upright.

"Hello ladies, I bought you all a drink." He placed them on the table.

Lydia picked one up, guzzled it in one swallow and put the barren tumbler back down.

Brie glanced at Darla. "Well, somebody is parched."

Lydia stood up. "I am ready to go." She snatched the guy's drink out of his hand, slammed it back and gave him the empty glass.

He inched back. "I'll get my car."

"No, that's not how it works," Brie snapped. "We pick you up; we take you home. That's the rule."

Lydia faced the guy. "Will you follow us?"

"I'll be in the yellow Corvette." He grabbed the keys out of his front pocket and bolted away.

"The girls picked up their handbags and headed for the exit. As they left, Lydia fell against the bouncer.

"Easy does it!" Brie grabbed her arm.

Darla grabbed the other arm. "We got you."

"I am so sorry..." Lydia burbled. "I lost my footing."

Rue took her hand. "Are you totally sure about this guy coming over?"

"I am quite sure," Lydia slurred.

When they arrived at the curb, the valet attendant grabbed their keys and stared at Rue. "I remember you!" He grinned. "I'll be right back with your vehicle." A sleek yellow Corvette pulled up alongside them and beeped the horn to get their attention.

163

"There is my man!" Lydia's head bobbed as she turned to the girls. "I am going to rock his world."

Brie looked at Darla with her eyebrow arched.

The valet driver pulled up and got out of the idling car. "I took extra good care of it for you." He winked at Rue.

"Like, thank you ever so!" She winked back.

Brie leaned into Darla. "If we don't get in this car soon, we're going to lose another one."

"And we definitely don't need that."

"Come on, girls," Brie bellowed. "Let's get into the car." She opened the driver's side door. "Mama's very tired and needs to hit the hay in a fast way, which by chance is the same way she's driving home."

All climbed in then zoomed off as the yellow Corvette kept pace.

"What a totally hot car," Rue uttered.

"What a truly hot man," Lydia muttered.

They leaned against each other and giggled.

When they arrived at the Alabaster Hotel, Brie pulled to the curb and stopped. "Let's make this quick! I need my beauty sleep."

"Then you'd so need to sleep forever!" Rue quickly opened the car door.

Lydia cackled. "We need to do this again." Her words muddled together. "I had a really good time."

"I have a feeling that the good time hasn't even met its climax," Brie said under her breath.

Lydia crawled out of the car with Rue's assistance. They hugged and kissed each other on the cheek as the guy walked up to them.

"I will talk to you tomorrow," Lydia slurred.

"Like, the minute you wake up," Rue ordered.

Lydia wrapped her arms around the man and was kissing him as Rue hopped into the car and closed the door.

Brie drove off. "Wow, she's a hussy!"

"Like, no she's not," Rue roared. "She's foreign."

"Lydia is supposed to be dating Logan Price, but has been with me and now with this guy." Darla's hands went up. "I've got to call a spade...a spade—"

"Or a tramp...a tramp," Brie added.

Rue smirked. "Nothing was totally said to me when I was Russ and way sleeping with everything in sight."

"That's different," Darla stated. "A man is mocked if he's not a stud, but a woman is ridiculed if she's a slut."

"Like, no double standard there," Rue quipped.

"Women have to set the tone," Brie remarked. "Even though they say it's a man's world, it's really a woman's and they run everything."

"Maybe Lydia is totally setting the tone for women around the world," Rue declared.

"She's definitely setting something..." Darla snickered. "Maybe it's the world record for most men in a given hour."

Rue huffed. "Like, whatever!"

"We've pretty much gotten all of the information we're going to get," Darla stated. "We really don't need to pretend we're her friends anymore."

"If you two seriously do not want to be friends with her, that's way fine," Rue countered. She'll so be mine, and I'll hang with her."

"Lydia is not a good influence on you, especially when she's under the influence," Brie cautioned. "There's something off about her. I can feel it."

"It's mostly her clothes, and I did feel it," Darla added.

"Like, I don't want to totally hear another snide remark about Lydia," Rue uttered. "Way get off and stay off her case."

Brie put the pedal to the metal. "Then case closed!"

Chapter 11

Large and intimidating was Prescott Chemicals as Simone pulled onto the side road leading to the entranceway. She drove alongside the fence of the twenty-five thousand square foot facility and watched the dense smoke that billowed out of the scattered stacks. Their clouds hung low over the ashen roof.

They should implement some green technology to rid our air of that cancerous smog.

Simone pulled into the cramped lot and circled around to look for an available space to park. After passing row upon row of cars, she found an empty slot and pulled into it. An uneasy feeling came over her. After turning off the car, she closed her eyes, took a deep breath and exhaled to calm the fluttering butterflies.

You're a journalist, and this is just an interview.

A sudden onset of nerves infiltrated every fiber of her being.

No, this one will be different. Very different.

Simone took another deep breath and slowly let it out.

Just remind yourself that this is for Jack.

She released her grip on the steering wheel.

With this interview, he'll have bona fide confidence in me from now on.

Simone picked up her handbag, opened the door and stood up. A gust of wind whooshed against her face, allowing a sweeping calm to envelop her. With poise and confidence, she crossed the parking lot.

I've got this!

166

She pushed open the double doors, entered Prescott Chemicals and marched up to the receptionist.

"Hello, my name is Simone Wellington and I have an appointment at 8:00am with Mr. Higgins."

"Please, have a seat in the waiting room, and I will let him know you're here," the receptionist said. "May I offer you a cup of coffee?"

"Thank you, but I've had my quota for the morning." Simone smiled, turned around and sat down. After picking up a magazine, she saw a shadow out of the corner of her eye and quickly looked up.

"Hi, Ms. Wellington, I'm Buford Higgins." Out came his hand. "You're still pretty as a picture."

Simone flinched then rose to her feet. He was an older man now; a shell of his former self. Excessive bags sagged under the eyes and his skin was roughhewn with a couple days' growth of beard. What little hair he had left was quite gray and baggy clothes hung on his scrawny frame.

"Thank you, Mr. Higgins." She reached out, briefly shook his hand then snatched it away. "That's very sweet of you to say. It's been a long time."

He grinned to expose some half-chipped and missing teeth. "Yeah, too long if you ask me."

Nobody's asking.

Buford's eyes moved up and down her body. "I see you've kept your nice shape." His hands formed an hour-glass. "A very nice shape indeed."

Simone cringed while closing up her jacket. "We should commence with the interview."

"Um...yeah," Buford murmured. "Did you bring a camera man?"

"I didn't," she admitted. "I wanted to get the story first then bring him down at a later date, just in case the interview doesn't fly with my boss. After all, she has the final decision."

"Oh, ok."

"That's the newspaper business," Simone uttered. "Just because I love the interview doesn't mean that everyone else will."

167

"Don't you worry," Buford assured her. "I'll make sure those people will like it. A no-holds-barred policy will be in effect. I'll answer all questions pitched to me."

Her eyes expanded. "Every question, no matter what?"

"Yep, every question," he replied.

Simone smiled. "It seems we're getting off on the right foot."

"Yeah, that's good because I'm left-footed," Buford said as another, even larger, tooth-challenged grin came over his face. "I'm just playing with you."

You'll never play with me. "Shall we begin?"

"Yep, just follow me." Buford turned around, walked to a side door and opened it. After heading down a flight of stairs and passing a large, lifeless machine, they entered a little room and proceeded to the far back.

Simone's comfort level dropped. *I wish more people were around. If this doesn't go well...it's not going to end well.*

"How is this space?" Buford asked. "Nobody will bother us here." He pulled out a chair and motioned for her to take a seat.

"I thought there'd be more..." She sat down. "I mean, others—"

"For what?" Buford blurted out.

"Just in case I wanted to get another perspective."

"Why do you need that?" His expression hardened. "What, I'm not enough?"

"No. I mean, yes. I, ah..." *I don't want to upset him. He might shut it all down.* "What I meant to say was that when someone else gives their perspective on a subject, they offer a differing opinion, which can give an interview some flavor; add some zest to it."

"I'm all the zest you need!" He yanked a chair out from under the table and plopped down.

Her lips quivered. "Yes, indeed. It was just a suggestion. I will do a singular interview."

"Yeah, you do that."

"I hope I didn't offend you," she stated. "That was not my intention."

168

Buford stayed quiet with his jaw clenched. After some time lapsed, his eyes moved toward Simone. "So, how does this all go down?"

"Excuse me?"

His face mellowed. "How does this go?"

Simone smiled and took a tape recorder out of her handbag. She placed it on the table between them. "I will be asking you a series of questions and you will give me your honest answers. I will chronicle the rest of it when I do the actual article."

"That's sounds easy enough."

"You just sit back and relax."

He slouched down in the chair and folded his arms.

"Are you ready to begin, Mr. Higgins?"

"What's with the formalities...we're friends, aren't we?"

She inhaled. "I feel we are."

He grinned. "Then you can call me Buford, and I'll call you Simone. As long as we're friends, and all."

She donned a slight smile. *I'll never make it out of here alive.* "May I begin the interview now?"

He nodded.

Simone edged forward and pushed the record button. "I'm here with Mr. Buford Higgins, and this interview is being conducted at Prescott Chemicals."

He sat up in his chair.

"Mr. Higgins, may I call you Buford?" Simone wanted to establish his identity.

"Yep..." He cleared his throat. "Ah...yeah—"

"Is it true that you and the proprietor, Mr. Henry Prescott, have developed a green alternative to the harsher chemical pesticides being sold on the market?"

"Yeah, but it was mostly my calculations that sustained the formula," he replied. "Henry was always busy with the daily grind. He did what he could."

"I was under the impression it would take a team of scientists to develop such a product."

"Ah...it usually does." His eyes dropped. "Henry isn't what you would call—a trusting individual. He didn't want anybody stealing the idea or our formulation for that matter. If it had fallen into our competitor's hands, it would've destroyed him and his company.

"Who else knows about it?" Simone inquired.

"Besides Henry and me; two other men."

"What's their role in it?"

"Mostly to ride the cash cow," Buford responded. "But money doesn't always buy silence."

"But it can sometimes rent an allegiance or lease an alliance."

"Not if greed becomes the successor."

"I've heard money is a blessing and a curse."

"So far for me it's been a blessing in disguise," he continued. "If not for working alone, I might not have had my Eureka moment."

"What was that?"

"During the homologous recombination of my eukaryotic organisms, the idea of cellular starvation through genome editing came to me. A genetically-engineered chromosomal mutation will initiate the onset of immunological deterioration, annihilating those blood-suckers."

"What?" Her eyebrows furrowed.

"Mosquitoes," he reacted. "With the introduction of genetically-modified viral pathogens, the cytotoxic cells have turned on themselves. Not only will they destroy the pesky insects, it'll eradicate their blood-carrying diseases too."

"Let me get this straight," she stated, gesturing with her hand. "You have tricked the immune system of a mosquito into attacking itself thus killing the insect?"

"Just the female species since they infect humans with their bite."

"I didn't know that."

170

"I've manipulated a DNA protein in the female to instigate a fatal antibody response from the host they feed on."

"How will you infect every one of them?"

"That's where the males come in," he replied. "They feed on the nectar of flowers. Since they won't be affected by the mutation, I've maneuvered key molecules within our product to infiltrate their reproductive system. When mating season begins, the newly infected females will be hunting for blood to assist with their eggs. Goodbye mother, goodbye offspring—"

"With one fell swoop."

"Yeah, to our competition." Buford smirked. "When the benefits of our product are revealed, our stock will soar sky-high along with the digits on our bank statements."

"Talk about hitting the motherlode."

"Yeah, we'll be raking in loads of money." He grinned. "You could, too. Just buy up some of our stocks over the next couple of weeks."

"It's a good thing I don't work for the FCC."

"Yeah, a very good thing," Buford quipped.

"Another very good thing is that your eco-friendly product has a dual purpose."

Yeah, with a pesticide to eradicate the many crop-destroying insects and an insecticide to annihilate mosquitoes carrying malaria, dengue, yellow fever and other diseases affecting people, it's what I would call a win-win situation."

"Have you given it a name?"

"Yeah, and I came up with it." Buford beamed. "It'll be marketed under the name Coincide."

"As in two things happening at the same time," Simone mentioned. "It's such smart branding."

"You'll get no argument from me."

She laughed. "Do you have any other products in the works?"

"Ah...I might."

"Would you care to elaborate?" Her lilt softened.

171

"Let's just say it's another natural creation."

She gazed into his eyes. "What's its intended purpose?"

"I, um...can't get into that right now."

"May I at least ask how long you've been working on it?"

"It was originated a long time ago..." Buford squirmed. "But I recently reformulated it."

"I wrote an article on New Product Development, also known as the Fuzzy Front End, and discovered that new chemical compounds are given a reference code." She leaned in. "Have you issued one to your new formulation?"

"Ah...not yet."

"You must call it something," she urged, upping the pressure.

"Um, it..." Buford inhaled and tipped his head down. "It's called..." He rubbed the back of his neck then exhaled. "We refer to it as TB4711."

Wow, he said it! Simone glowed. *Now it's time to close.* "When reformulating, did you add any man-made or should I say, synthetic ingredients to it?"

Buford fidgeted in his chair. "Why?"

"When preparing for this interview, my research uncovered some information regarding TB4711—"

"What information?"

"I found that several young men have suffered severe reactions to the formula and died."

"Who told you that?"

"You did!"

"Listen to me, damn it," he barked, pointing his gnarled finger. "I don't know what you're up to, but this line of questioning is for crap. I invited you down to interview me about our green pesticide, but instead you seem to be railroading me for some reason or another. It stops here." He slammed his fist onto the table.

She jerked. Simone knew there was no way of stopping it; not with the questions she was about to ask. "Mr. Higgins, I've found out that not only is TB4711 not a completely organic preparation, but it's being manufactured for a diabolical purpose—"

"I told you to quiet down!" He gritted his teeth. "This interview is over."

Simone couldn't end the interview until she got what was needed. "Isn't it true that you and your cronies are conspiring to use TB4711 on the President of the United States?"

"I said this interview is over," Buford howled as rage engulfed his face. He jumped up from his chair and stormed toward her.

She took flight.

After several laps around the oblong table, Buford stopped. "I'll get you sooner or later, bitch."

Simone stood across the table with her heart pounding. Even in stilettos, she held her own.

"I tried to play nice with you." He leaned his hands on the table and panted.

"Play nice! Is that what you just said?"

"Since I'm not deaf, that's what you heard."

"The only reason you agreed to do this interview was in the hopes of sleeping with me."

He wiped his dripping forehead. "It's called tit for tat, honey."

"Do you really think I'm so desperate that I'd trade sex for some information?" she asked, swinging her head from side to side. "I have so much more self-respect and self-esteem than the need for a story."

"Well, now that the offer is on the table..." Buford leered. "How bad do you want the truth?"

"You are so pathetic!" She slung her handbag over her shoulder. "I'm leaving."

"Not before I get that tape recorder." He reached out. "Just slide it to me."

"Goodbye." Simone turned around.

Buford vaulted onto the table and lunged at her. "You scheming bitch! I said give it to me."

They plummeted to the floor.

She thrashed about while screaming for help.

"I should've of done this a long time ago." He tore at her blouse.

"Stop!" Simone shouted out as she clawed his face; gouging out gullies of flesh in the process.

Buford roared. "I'll kill you!" He rubbed his hands against the bleeding wounds.

Simone wriggled loose. "You bastard!" She kicked him in the ribs and ran away.

He hopped up. "You're dead, bitch!" he hollered, hurrying after her.

As she ran down the hall, Buford clenched onto her arm and hurled her into the wall. Simone's limp body collapsed to the floor with a thud and remained motionless. After opening a nearby door that housed supplies, he grabbed a handful of hair, dragged her into it and tossed her body by some cleaning agents.

"Look at the famous Simone Wellington now." He laughed out loud. After rifling through her handbag, he yanked out the tape recorder, along with her cell phone and threw the rest of it on top of Simone. As she moaned, he shut the door, locked it and bolted upstairs to the laboratory.

A few minutes later, the lab door flung open and startled him. "Have you seen Lydia Reome anywhere?" Henry asked. "She should've been here by now. It's close to 9:40am," he squawked, staring at his watch. "Women..." His hands went up. "They always have to make an entrance."

Buford snickered. "I warned you."

"What's wrong with your face?"

"Nothing—"

"Well, if it's nothing then why don't you get Arvin Horton and drive over to Lydia's hotel just in case there's a situation," Henry demanded. "Her application is sitting on my desk, so get the room number and pay a little visit."

"I can't," Buford uttered. "I've got a situation here."

"Listen," Henry barked. "You'll definitely have a situation here if you don't get your ass in gear and get that woman." He snapped his fingers. "As a matter of fact, bring her to me immediately when you get back. I've got to make sure she understands the hours."

"But, Henry—"

"Don't but me," he growled. "Just move it."

"Ok!" Buford backed up.

"While you're gone, I'm giving the crew the rest of the day off," he grumbled. "Something feels off, today. And my bursitis is acting up."

Buford nodded his head.

"Don't just stand there bobbing your head, let's get going," Henry roared. "Move it!"

Buford scrambled out of the room, barreled down the stairs missing several steps and ran out the front door. He leaped into his car and raced out of the parking lot. After driving like a maniac for two miles, he slammed on his brakes which caused the tires to squeal.

"Arvin, that friend of yours is here," his mother screeched from the front porch.

"Ok, Ma...I'm coming." He darted out the front door.

"Will you be home for dinner?"

"I don't know, Ma," Arvin howled, opening the car door. "Just leave it in the stove." He soared onto the seat and slammed the door shut. "Go!"

Buford stomped the pedal to the floor and the car peeled away.

"Ma's been driving me nuts with her constant squawking," Arvin complained. "I couldn't wait to get the hell out of there." His legs shook. "Where're we going?"

"We've got orders from Henry," Buford responded. "There's a problem."

"I figured that after you told me to bring my gun and to make sure it's loaded."

"That Lydia chick I told you about, the one Logan insisted Henry should hire. Well, she never showed up this morning."

"Dames, they're not for business."

175

"I've got an even bigger problem."

Arvin raised an eyebrow. "Yeah?"

"Yeah," Buford declared. "Remember me telling you about that reporter from the Washington Tribune, the one who flirted with me at Jonestown when we went to that twentieth year what-cha-ma-call-it?"

"Uh-huh." Arvin nodded with his mouth open.

"I invited her down here this morning to interview me."

"About what?"

"About nothing," Buford retorted. "I wanted to get her on my turf and flirt with her. I was gonna' ask her out to dinner then maybe back to my house for a drink."

Arvin exposed a dim-witted grin.

"Instead of that happening, she started asking me questions about TB4711 and our plans regarding its use...and she was tape recording it."

"What'd you do?"

"When the interview fell apart, I jumped her and beat her down. Then I took the recorder and put her in the supply closet across from our meeting room." He turned his head to show the wound on the left side of the face. "This is what that stupid bitch did to me."

"Damn!" Arvin rumbled. "That looks like hell."

"Hell hath no fury like a woman scorned."

Arvin laughed. "Hell hasn't met a man's ego yet."

"You've got that right." Buford pulled up to the curb and they got out of the car.

"Let's do this!" Arvin plowed through the hotel doors.

"She's in room 604."

"May I help you gentlemen?" asked the concierge.

"No," Arvin grumbled as he held his stride.

"We've got it." Buford kept pace behind him.

176

Both men stopped at the elevator and together hit the up button.

"That guy just let us by without a hitch." Buford grinned.

Arvin balled up his fist. "He didn't have a choice."

When the doors opened, they took the elevator to the sixth floor and went to Lydia's room.

"She hung a 'Do Not Disturb' sign," Arvin heckled.

"Oh, she'll be disturbed once we get a hold of her." Buford knocked on the door, but received no answer. He knocked again much harder.

"Let me pound on it."

"Look, there's a maid down the hall." Buford pointed. "We should go butter her up."

They traipsed toward her.

Arvin stopped short. "Whoa, she's really old."

Buford leaned in. "So, flirt with her anyways."

"Damn, my Ma looks like a youngster compared to her," Arvin muttered out of the corner of his mouth. "I can't flirt with an old broad."

"I've got to do everything." Buford rolled his eyes. He approached her. "My friend and I left our key card in the room and we feel kind of weird asking you to open our door."

"Oh, don't feel embarrassed, dear, people do it all the time," the maid said. "Where is your room?"

Buford pointed. "It's the second door on the left."

"Come with me." She led them to room 604. "I'll open it for two handsome young men."

"Thank you, ma'am." Buford watched her unlock it.

"There you go!" The maid swung open the door. "Do you want it cleaned today?"

"No," Arvin blurted out.

"We're bachelors, ma'am, and are comfortable with a more lived-in look," Buford added.

177

The maid smiled. "Well, if you do need anything, just ask for Mildred." She pinched Arvin's butt and scuttled away.

"Whoa, she just goosed me!" His voice jumped an octave.

Buford patted him on the shoulder. "Just think, that's the most action you've had in some time. I mean, not counting your cousin, Willie Lou."

"Shut up before I cook your goose."

"Who're you talking smack to?"

"You," Arvin growled through gritted teeth.

Buford stepped back. "Save your mad-dog routine for the girl."

Arvin nodded. "Let's find her."

"I'll check the bedroom." Buford walked down the hallway. He looked into the room. "She's here...in bed."

Arvin came in. "Whoa, she has a man with her." He winced. "Phew, it smells like a distillery in here."

"Wake up, sleepy-heads!" Buford kicked the bed. "It's time to get up," he shouted at the top of his lungs.

Lydia opened her eyes. "Who are you?" She sat up and pulled the sheet up to her chin.

"I'm Buford Higgins, the guy who's supposed to be your co-worker."

Lydia scowled. "Why are you both in my bedroom?"

"When you didn't show up for work, Henry became concerned. He asked me to come here and see what the problem was."

"Well, you can both leave because I am not coming in to work." Lydia put her head back down. "Breaking the law is not on my resume so get somebody else."

Buford yanked her out of bed by the hair, pulled his gun out and forced her to put on some clothes. "Unfortunately sweetheart, you signed a non-disclosure agreement which states you're the sole property of Henry Prescott so get a move on."

"What's going on?" The man sat up in the bed and looked at Lydia. "Who're these guys?"

Arvin darted toward the bed, swung his gun and cold-cocked the guy with it. "That's who we are!" He wiped the blood off his revolver with the bed sheet. "That oughta' shut him up for a while." His firearm was raised. "Let's move it, doll-face, or you'll be next."

"I am hurrying." Lydia threw on a blouse then slid on her heels. "You did not have to hit him." She grabbed her purse off the chair.

"You're right." Arvin chuckled. "I could've killed him instead."

She gasped.

Let's blow this joint," Buford stated. He grabbed one of Lydia's arms and Arvin grasped the other. They dragged her out the door and onto the elevator.

"Please, let go..." She squirmed. "You are hurting me."

"Not on your life, sister," Arvin remarked.

"Listen to me," Buford uttered. "When we get out of this contraption, you better have a smile on your pretty face. We're going to walk through the lobby, out the front door and get into that green Chevy parked in front." His scowled face edged in. "If you do anything to draw attention, I'll drop you where you stand. Not to mention I'll do the same to anybody else that gets in our way. Understood?"

"I understand," Lydia muttered with her head down.

"Look me in the eye and say it." Buford shook her.

"Lydia lifted up her head as the tears flowed down her cheeks. "I understand."

Buford sneered. "Shut off the damn water works!"

The elevator rang.

"Ok, smile everybody," Buford quipped. "Let's look like we're having fun."

The doors opened. They walked off through the lobby, exited the building and got into the car. They drove to Prescott Chemicals and the men brought Lydia to Henry's office.

"Here's your sweet angel," Buford declared. He flung her down into a chair. "She's hung-over and had a man in her bed."

"Lydia, were you planning to come in today, at any time, to help with perfecting our formula?" Henry asked.

179

"I have decided that I am going back to France to pursue other endeavors," she replied. "I am leaving Logan and thought my employment here would be a distraction, so I decided to make a clean break."

"I see." Henry turned around and faced the window. "It makes perfect sense to me."

Buford eyes broadened. "Huh?"

"I was wondering, since you're already here and there's been no harm done, would you consider staying a couple of hours and taking a look at our formula?" Henry queried. "Another pair of eyes just might do the trick."

Lydia exhaled. "Did you just say, 'no harm done'?" She raised herself up from the chair. "You sent two men up to my hotel room wielding guns. As I slept naked, one of your men dragged me out of bed by my hair while your other man bashed my guest in the head, most likely killing him. From there, I was forced to dress, kidnapped at gunpoint and brought here against my will!"

"Like I said, no harm done," Henry reiterated.

"There will be, Mr. Prescott, when I call the police," Lydia stated.

Arvin and Buford jerked.

Henry held out his hand toward them both. "What do you plan on telling them, Ms. Reome? Would it be that these two men came to your hotel and escorted you to your first day of work?" He walked over to his desk and ripped her application in half. "Wise up, honey, this is what's going to take place. Buford will show you to the lab and together you will perfect the formula. If that happens, maybe—just maybe—I'll let you live. If, on the other hand, you refuse, or destroy the elixir—well, let's just say, since nobody on God's green earth knows where you are, I'll make sure it stays that way. You will become a permanent fixture here. Did I make myself perfectly clear?"

"No," Lydia responded. "It will never happen."

"Never..." Henry remarked. "Are you sure about that?"

Lydia crossed her arms and looked at the wall.

180

"Have it your way, honey." Henry shrugged. "Buford, lock her up somewhere. A few days in the dark without food or water should change her mind."

"Arvin, grab her and follow me," Buford clamored. "I know exactly where to put this indignant bitch." He walked out of the office, went down the stairs to the bottom floor and up to the closet door. He unlocked and opened it so all could see the woman lying on the floor.

Lydia gasped.

"Who's that?" Arvin's eyes expanded.

"Why, it's Lydia's new playmate," Buford retorted. "She can see what'll happen to her if there's no cooperation. Throw her in there," he commanded.

"Are you sure?"

Buford raised his gun. "Did I just tell you to do something?"

"Whoa, who're you pointing that at?"

Buford lowered his gun. "I asked you to toss her into the supply closet."

"Ok," Arvin grunted. "You act like I do this every day." He heaved her into the closet.

"See how easy that was?" Buford closed and locked the door. "Even a degenerate could do it."

"You better watch your mouth," Arvin ordered through clenched teeth.

Buford lifted the gun up again. "Is that a threat?"

"No!" Arvin stepped back. "I swear on my mother's grave." His left hand went up.

"I just saw your mother when I picked you up." Buford busted out with laughter. "And it's your right hand that's put up when you avow an oath."

Arvin's forehead wrinkled. "I hope those broads didn't hear you—"

"Loosen up!"

"You're not supposed to drop character until you're fully out of earshot."

181

"We were far enough away..." Buford reached around Arvin's shoulders. "Besides, I couldn't hold a straight face with that remark."

"Yeah, that was a good one."

"C'mon," Buford uttered. "I need to work on the formula."

They scurried up the stairs and entered the lab. Henry was leaning against the work station where the beakers were housed.

"Logan is quite pissed," he growled with his nostrils flared. "I told him about Lydia and he's on his way down. I'm not in the mood to deal with his shenanigans. Is that understood?"

Both nodded.

Henry edged toward Buford. "I don't care how you fix this God-forsaken formula, but get it done," he barked as the spit flew from his quaking lips.

The phone rang.

Henry leaned over and hit the speaker button. "Yes?"

"Mr. Prescott, Mr. Price is on line two," the receptionist said. "He tried to reach you on your private line."

"Thanks, Kitty...put him through."

"Ok, sir."

Henry waved his hands at Arvin. "Quick! Go and shut the lab door. I don't want this broadcasted through the entire building."

He turned and bolted.

Henry pushed the blinking red button. "What's up?"

"I need to have TB4711 ready to go by tomorrow morning," Logan howled.

"I just told Buford to get this cockamamie crap perfected and ready for a final trial run tonight," Henry uttered.

"Does he know what he's doing?" Logan asked.

Buford spoke up. "I've got one more element to formalize which should alter the appurtenance to decussate the blood-brain barrier and—"

"Hell what?" Logan crowed.

182

Henry banged his fist on the counter. "Buford!"

He jerked. "It should be fixed within a few hours."

"Not should or could, but will..." Logan demanded. "It will be fixed!"

"Ok," Buford bleated. "You will have it soon."

"That's what I wanted to hear," Logan stated. "I'll be there soon."

A dial tone echoed throughout the room.

Chapter 12

Rue paced back and forth, clutching her cell phone between her fingers. After hitting the redial button yet another time, she put it to her ear. It rang the usual four times then went to voicemail. With a stomp of her foot, out came a huff.

"What's up?" Darla asked.

"Like, I've called Lydia several times with no answer," she replied. "Something is seriously wrong. I can so feel it in my gut." She placed a hand over her stomach. "What should I totally do?"

Darla closed the fashion magazine she was reading and tossed it on the coffee table. "First, you need to back the hell off the carpet before it's worn into scraps." She leaned to her side and crossed her legs. "Second, being a detective and a woman, you should trust your instinct...otherwise known as female intuition."

"You're way right!" Rue snapped her fingers. "Like, we should get dressed and majorly go over to her hotel room."

"We?" Darla questioned. "I don't remember forming those two letters...let alone saying them."

Rue hopped onto the sofa. "Totally come with me, please," she pleaded. "Pretty please with cherries on top!"

Darla licked her lips. "I'll go with you on this expedition, but I've got one condition—"

"Like, what?"

"I need a promise that after our sleuthing, we'll stop off at Grandma's Ice Cream Parlor where you'll buy me a big double chocolate sundae with swaths of whipped cream, walnuts, a cherry and lots of gooey hot fudge."

"Hot fudge..." Brie entered the living room while scratching her derriere. "I'm so there!"

"Oh, look, sleeping booty," Darla remarked. "I see you've decided to join the living."

Brie pointed at the two of them. "If that's what alive looks like, I'd rather go back to my bedroom and crawl into dead."

Darla smirked. "Aren't you afraid someone might put a stake in your heart?"

"No, dear," Brie replied. "Remember, I don't have one." She turned aside. "Now back to my crypt."

"No," Rue blurted out. "You so need to get dressed and go with us to see if Lydia's alive. Like, she hasn't returned my messages."

"Please, that nasty, filthy tramp," Brie snarled. "You know she's doing the nasty all over that hotel room and just doesn't want to stop, especially to answer the telephone. If I was the Alabaster Hotel, in lieu of cleaning her suite, I'd don a Hazmat suit, crack the door and hurl in a Molotov cocktail to sanitize the bacterial, venereal or viral infections she has dispersed about from spreading throughout the complex, thus keeping our fair city clean."

"Are you finished, or is there more hatred that needs to be spewed? Darla asked.

Brie stuck up her nose. "No, I am quite finished—for now that is."

"Lydia is way important to our case," Rue uttered. "We should all go and totally check it out."

"As the best detective out of us three, my extensive expertise would be of great help," Brie boasted. "I also want one of those hot fudge thing-a-ma-jigs."

"Like, duly noted!" Rue jumped from the couch. "It's time to move and groove." She sprinted toward the hallway while the other two moved at a much slower pace.

When dressed, they got into the car and headed toward the Alabaster Hotel. Once inside, the girls took the elevator to the sixth floor, got off and went up to Lydia's room.

"Whoa!" Darla balked. "The door is open."

Rue pulled out her gun and with her tactical training in mind, entered first. After scanning the kitchen, she leaned against a wall then peeked around the corner. She motioned to Darla that the coast was clear and to come in. Brie entered last.

185

Silence engulfed the suite as Rue crept further in. She scoured the living room, swung her head in the direction of the dining room, placed her backside against another wall then signaled to Darla, who inched inside. Brie trailed closely behind.

Rue wormed along the wall until she caught sight of the bathroom. She snaked her head around and searched the room with her eyes. Since it was clear, she crouched down, stuck the barrel of the gun out where Darla and Brie could see it and motioned for them to bypass her.

Once the girls got into position, Rue skirted by and put her shoulder to the molding outside the bedroom doorway. After angling her head, she peered in. The curtains were drawn and the room was bathed in darkness. She turned and signaled to her partners. After scrambling to the opposite side of the doorway, they looked at one another then Darla nodded. Brie leaned in and shouted.

"Lydia, are you there?"

There was no answer.

"Like, it's the girls!" Rue yelled.

They heard a moan.

"Are you hurt?" Darla hollered.

More moaning emanated.

Rue reached her hand around and flicked on the light. Each darted into the bedroom with their guns poised for an altercation.

They heard a groan.

"Whoa, there's a bloody, naked man on the bed," Darla shrieked.

Rue rushed toward him, snatched the sheet and covered his masculine parts. "Like, are you ok?"

"I'd say not," Darla quipped.

Brie walked up. "The bathroom is clear."

As the man groaned, Rue moved his hair away from the gaping wound in his forehead. "Darla, totally grab me a wet, warm washcloth."

186

"Sure." She dashed into the bathroom.

"I'll call 911." Brie dialed the phone on the night stand.

Darla came out with the moist cloth. "Here..." The water oozed from her fingers. "I wet a hand towel instead because I didn't know how bad it was."

Rue snatched it and dabbed the blood. "Like, he's going to need some major stitches."

"Ouch." Darla winced.

"Sir, can you totally hear me?" Rue cradled his head.

"Y—yeah," he slurred.

Darla leaned in. "What hurts on you?"

"M—my head hurts re—real bad." He lifted a trembling hand toward the wound.

"Sweetie, don't do that," Rue uttered, pushing his arm away. She adjusted the towel. "I'll so take care of it."

He grimaced, but managed to crack a partial smile.

"Besides your head, does anything else hurt? Darla asked.

"No," was the faint reply.

Brie came up. "An ambulance is on its way."

Darla sat on the edge of the bed. "Would you be able to answer a few questions?"

He nodded his head with his eyes shut.

"Do you know where Lydia is?"

"She was taken by two men," he mumbled.

Rue gasped. "Oh my God!"

"Do you know why they took Lydia?" Brie queried.

His eyes opened. "The shorter man with the strong hillbilly accent said something about her work—"

"Son-of-a-gun, they took her down to Prescott Chemicals," Darla blurted out. She sprang off the bed. "I hear sirens!"

"I'll go down and get them." Brie rushed out of the bedroom.

187

"I need my clothes," the wounded guy said. "I'm sure they'll call my wife."

Darla balked. "You're married?"

"Yeah," he groaned.

"Like, grab his pants." Rue pointed to a nearby chair.

"Really?" Darla snarled. "He's a cheater!"

"And you so wore a hideous brown dress with grody brown shoes out in public..." Rue's face rumpled. "Lest we forget what Derek totally did in this very room?"

"Ok, I get it!" Darla announced. "There'll be no more stones thrown at glass houses today," she stated. "You do know he shouldn't be moved with a head wound, right?"

"Help me, please," came his plea.

"I can't believe I'm aiding and abetting this guy."

"And totally dressing him, too," Rue added.

"Are you serious?" Darla grimaced. "He's very nude."

"Like, duh..." Rue enunciated both words. "That's why I so asked for his pants."

"I'm not touching his underwear."

Rue glared. "Then he'll totally go commando!"

Darla huffed then dashed over and grabbed the jeans. After kneeling down, she slid the opening over his feet and pulled them up to his knees. "I can't go any farther so he needs to stand."

Rue helped the wounded guy to his feet. Once he was up, Darla closed her eyes and yanked the trousers to the middle of his thighs.

Rue looked down. "I so cannot hold him up forever."

"I'm doing my best," Darla yelled. She tugged again, but they stopped just below his butt.

"Like, today?"

Darla puffed, flung her hands around his backside and gripped the top of his jeans. She emitted a loud grunt, jerked them over his rear and banged her face against his manhood. As her head snapped back, Brie entered the bedroom.

"What the—"

"I can pull them up from here." The injured guy reached down.

As the two paramedics wheeled the gurney in, Darla fell to the side and crawled away.

"We'll take it from here," one of the uniformed men said.

Rue looked at the injured guy and winked. "Like, make sure they hook you up to the majorly good stuff."

He winked back as the paramedics assisted him onto the gurney.

Back on her feet, Darla said, "I'm glad that's over."

"Totally!" Rue agreed.

As the paramedics maneuvered the gurney away, the victim smiled and waved to the girls before it was rolled out.

Brie turned toward Darla and threw up her hand. "I don't even want to know what that exhibition was about."

"It's not what you think—"

"Darla, save it for somebody who cares." Brie swung her head around and walked toward the bedroom door. "Right now we have statements to give and a Lydia to rescue."

"Like, totally," Rue uttered. She followed behind with Darla on her tail.

After the reports were filled out, the detectives left the hotel, got into the car and sped south with their sights set on Prescott Chemicals. When they arrived, the parking lot was near empty.

"Where is everybody?" Darla asked. "It's the middle of the work day."

"Something major is going down," Rue blurted out.

Brie shut off the engine and popped the trunk. "Grab your bags, girls."

Darla unhooked her seatbelt. "It's time to female down and man up."

"Like, it gives a whole new meaning to going through the change." Rue opened her door.

189

All three jumped out of the car, grabbed a duffle bag along with a garment bag and hopped back in.

With a slam of the door, Darla said, "Brie, since you're a virgin, you should go through the change first."

"Please, if you two brain-dead bimbos can do it, I will have no problem."

"Like, we'll see," Rue countered. "Let's so do this!"

The girls disrobed, closed their eyes and remained silent. A few seconds later, each one had metamorphosed into a guy.

Derek slapped the dashboard. "Man, who won?"

"The smartest one," Bren crowed.

Russ grinned. "So, it was totally me!"

Laughter filled the car.

"Let's throw our uniforms on," Derek stated.

Russ opened his garment bag. "Like, why do we so have to be OSHA dudes?"

"It's a chemical plant," Bren spoke up. "We're here investigating a workplace safety issue that was lodged by an employee."

"It's a way grody disguise," Russ grumbled. "Why can't we be totally cool and enter as cops and arrest somebody?"

"And who should we arrest?" Derek asked.

"Duh!" Russ retorted. "Like, the prettiest chick we see."

Bren and Derek shook their heads.

The detectives grabbed their duffle bags and walked through the doors of Prescott Chemicals. As they moved across the lobby, Bren whispered, "Remember, we are professionals, and above all else, I do the talking."

Derek and Russ rolled their eyes.

They approached the receptionist and Bren greeted her then went into his spiel. When he finished, she picked up the phone and pressed a button. "Hello, Mr. Prescott, there are three OSHA agents here to examine our workplace conditions and..." She stopped. Her facial expression changed. "Yes, sir, I will be right up." After putting the phone down, she stood and placed her hand out. "Please, have a seat in our lobby. I will return momentarily."

The detectives tipped their heads then watched as the woman hurried up a flight of stairs.

"She's gone," Derek said. "Let's get to work."

"Like, we need to find that vat and so grab a sample," Russ uttered.

"Follow me!" Bren took off. He ran around the corner, opened a solitary door and with the other two in tow, trotted down the stairs.

"It's so quiet down here." Derek kept pace.

"Even this machine that totally made all the grody racket has shut down." Russ touched it.

"Listen!" Bren held up his hand. "Do you hear that thumping noise?" He walked on.

"Way, I so hear it," Russ responded.

Derek pointed. "Somebody's banging on that door."

Bren leaned against it. "Who's there?"

Nobody answered, but they could hear muffled sounds.

Bren grabbed the knob. "It's locked."

"The door swings inward," Derek noted. "Russ, kick it down."

"Totally!" He cocked the leg back, rammed his foot against the door and busted it open.

Derek dashed in. "Whoa, man, its Lydia and—"

"That's Simone Wellington from the Washington Tribune!" Bren bent down on his knee. "I read your column every day." He helped her up.

"Oh, thank you." She brushed herself off then lifted her purse off the floor.

As Derek helped Lydia, she asked, "Why are you here?"

"We are detectives," he replied. "The night we met at the Back Alley Bar, we were conducting surveillance on the two men you sat with." He turned. "This guy here is Rue's brother, Russ."

"Like, it's way cool meeting you," he uttered. "My sister totally talks about you a lot."

"You speak just like her," Lydia said.

Russ grinned. "We're major California brats."

Lydia smiled. "Is she also a detective?"

"Enough with the socializing!" Bren interrupted. "We need to get out of here before we're discovered."

Derek turned around and pointed. "We've got to go in this direction."

"Follow me and stay quiet." Bren took the lead.

"I'll so pick up the rear." Russ fell to the back of the line to keep an eye out for signs of trouble.

They walked in a single file and suddenly heard footsteps trouncing down the grated stairs. Bren spun around and motioned for everybody to go behind an enormous machine that housed several mounted instruments. As they fled into hiding, the advancing paces became louder until—"

"Jack!" Simone exclaimed. She sprang out of hiding and sprung up to hug him.

"Wow, are we glad to see you," Bren remarked as the rest of the group came out and surrounded them.

"Like, you got here lickety-split," Russ quipped.

"I was half way here when Raymond called me to say that you guys were coming down with some damning evidence," Jack said. "You see, without her knowledge, I had a GPS tracker attached to Simone's car—"

"What?"

He looked at her. "When Stan McCall informed me that he had traced a call that came from Prescott Chemicals yesterday morning, I went for a listen, but nothing was there. You hadn't turned on the recording device for some reason and it sent a red flag up in my mind. My gut told me to follow your every move, so I had a friend place the device on your car."

"Really, you did that?" Simone asked.

192

"Yes, and I'm glad I did," Jack replied. "Imagine my surprise when I came into work this morning and discovered that your car was at Prescott Chemicals."

"I wanted to help you crack your case," Simone stated. "That's why I didn't push the button down to record the conversation. Buford wouldn't have told you squat, and therefore you wouldn't be able to arrest him. I knew with the way he pines after me that I could get him to open up, and that's what I did, until he took my tape recorder away."

"He and his cronies are very dangerous men," Jack declared. "Next time, it might not go as well and you could get seriously hurt, or worse—"

"Oh, you can count on worse," Henry Prescott shouted. He was perched at the top of the stairs with Buford, Arvin and Logan standing next to him.

"Everybody, split up," Jack yelled. He and Simone ran one way while Derek grabbed Lydia and followed Bren and Russ in the opposite direction.

"Get them!" Henry barked as he forced Arvin and Buford down the stairs. He and Logan turned around and ran.

Bren led his group around the corner and came to another hallway. As they fled down it, he noticed a door with a maintenance sign. He opened it and motioned for them to go inside.

"This room totally hoards the electrical guts to this baby," Russ uttered.

Derek pointed. "Look, there's a service elevator over there."

Bren snapped his fingers. "I've got an idea, albeit a crazy one." He tossed his duffle bag onto a small metal table.

"Anything at this point will do," Derek quipped.

"First, I want to safeguard Lydia." Bren turned his head. "There's a restroom over there." He pointed toward the area then looked at her. "I want you to go inside and lock the door, and do not under any circumstance open it until you hear one of our voices telling you that the coast is clear. We'll pile a couple of those big crates against it for your safety."

193

"I will." She scurried over, closed the door behind her and locked it. The guys stacked a few items in front to conceal the room.

"That's good." Bren stepped aside. "Now follow me." He hurried back to the table.

"What's up?" Derek stood readied.

"Russ, I want you to change into Rue, and put on the sexiest thing in your bag," Bren ordered. "Once dressed, pull out a purse and put your gun in it. Next, take the service elevator up to the floor above, go around the corner, get on the personnel elevator and ride it down." His hands were expressive. "When you get off, apply your hips and walk for your life. Those morons will see you and head you off, so make up some cock-and-bull story to keep their attention. With their backs to us, Derek and I will sneak around and take them by total surprise. Can you do this?"

He grinned then removed his clothes and shut his eyes. A female bubbled forth. "So, you want me to become utterly gorgeous then sashay down the hall to entice a man or two, and from there, work my charm, so their attention stays focused totally on me?"

"Yes, basically the same thing you do every day," Bren remarked.

Rue smirked then yanked some items out of the duffle bag and dressed. After sliding on a pair of heels and running both hands throughout her blonde curls to add a sexy fluff, she placed the weapons into a purse then placed a hand on her hip. "Will this majorly work?"

Bren gawked. "Ah, that will most definitely work." A gulp was heard.

"Like, even without a stitch of makeup, I'm still stunning!"

Derek smiled. "As long as you stun those fools out there—"

"That's why I so have my Taser in with my revolver." Rue flaunted her clutch. "I'm now way stunning—"

"Ouch!" Derek whipped out his hand.

She gave it a soft high-five.

"I don't want to break up your tea party, but I do want you to work," Bren spoke up.

194

"Like, you're such a major party pooper!" Rue ran her finger along his chest.

Bren grabbed and pretended to bite it.

Derek popped his head in between them. "Ah, can we get some work done?" He stuffed a gun down the back of his pants and covered it over with his shirt. "Let's do this!"

As they hastened to the elevator, Bren pushed the button. "Be careful."

"Totally!" Rue winked.

"Don't worry, baby, we've got your back," Derek stated.

The doors opened. "Like, you guys always do." She got on and faced them. Rue gave a coy smile and a little wave. "I'll so see you boys on the other side."

They nodded as their partner disappeared.

The elevator grinded its way up and stopped. She waited for the doors to open. When they did, Rue walked off, entered the other one, took it down to the floor below and got off. She jutted out her bosom and slinked down the hall until the two men came into view. As foretold, they walked toward her.

"Who do we have here?" the first man asked with a grin.

The second man sniggered. "My future wife."

Rue shuddered. *Like, hell!*

"Hi, I'm Buford." His eyes moved up and down her body. "What's your name?"

Out came a breathy voice. "I'm Rue."

"I'm Arvin." He leered at her. "Do you work here?"

She narrowed her eyes and raised her cheeks, "Like, I'm supposed to be picking my brother up who works here, but I got so lost." She sniffled and quivered her lips.

"Ah, don't get yourself all upset..." Buford yanked a handkerchief from his pocket and handed it to her. "I'll help you find him." He leaned in.

"We'll both help you find your brother." Arvin edged closer.

195

As she dabbed her eye, Rue noticed Bren's gun barrel as it inched out from the corner of a wall. "You two are totally sweet." She got cozy with them.

Bren put his gun barrel out a second time. Then a third.

Rue jerked. "Like, the strap on my heel broke." She bent down then fell to the floor.

"Drop your weapons!" Bren shouted.

Buford and Arvin turned around and pulled out their guns. They dived to the ground, slithered behind various machines and fired off some bullets.

As rounds were exchanged, Rue crawled behind a concrete pole and brandished her gun.

"Give up!" Derek yelled. "You're backed against the wall with no way out."

"You give up!" Buford hollered.

"Neither of you will get out of here alive!" Bren roared. "So, put down your weapons and surrender."

"We'll die first!" Arvin howled.

Rue eked her head out and spotted Buford. She took aim and shot him.

"I've been hit," Buford screeched, grasping his leg.

More gunfire was traded as bullets penetrated a boiler, flew into walls, whizzed off a vat and struck pumps and pipes. Another barrage hit a huge console and caused sparks to ignite. An explosion erupted and created a ball of flame. A fiery heat immediately followed.

"Everybody down!" Derek screamed. "Get close to the ground."

"Arvin, get over here and help me you dim-witted fool..." Buford wriggled on the floor. "Can't you see that I'm a sitting duck, you numbskull?"

"It's time to surrender!" Bren bellowed.

As the wall behind him blazed with flames, Arvin shot off a round and scurried over to Buford. He grabbed an arm and dragged his wounded friend behind another piece of equipment.

196

"It's time to pack it up!" Derek yelled.

"No way!" Buford yelped.

As they discharged a barrage of bullets, Bren and Derek darted up the hallway and ducked behind an apparatus that had lights radiating from it.

Thick smoke engulfed the area as Rue ran to a nearby wall and put her back against it. After lowering down, she inched along the floor toward the maintenance room.

Another explosion sent debris into the air.

Oh, my God! Rue's face was buried between her folded arms.

Alarms were activated.

As the water bombarded her, Rue reached up, turned the knob and pushed open the door. Once inside, she dropped down her wet clothes and changed back into a man. He dressed, ran over and removed the cargo that was placed in front of the bathroom door.

"Like, Lydia, its Russ." His voice held urgency. "The coast is totally clear, so unlock the door."

When it opened, she threw her arms around his neck. "Thank God!"

Russ broke loose and grabbed her hand. He headed toward the maintenance elevator and hit the button with his fist. "I'm totally bringing you to our car for safe keeping."

Lydia nodded.

The elevator grinded to a halt. They got on, went to the first floor, jumped out and ran outside. Once at the car, Russ opened the door and placed her inside. "Like, lock the door and stay put until we get back." He reached down, lifted his pant leg, pulled out a small pistol and handed it to her. "So take this just in case a little trouble brews."

She balked. "I have never held one."

He leaned in. "It totally shoots blanks."

"Blanks?" Her eyes squinted.

"Like, it's a fake bullet called a wad," Russ uttered. "I way make my own, so there's no danger if my gun is taken or used on me."

Lydia smiled.

197

"It's totally for show purposes only." He grinned. "Like, all sound with no pound."

Bren and Derek stormed out of Prescott Chemicals with Buford and Arvin in handcuffs. They were all soaking wet.

"That was majorly fast, dudes," Russ quipped. "Like, I thought the second explosion would've slowed you way down."

Derek smirked. "Not when the joint's a-rockin' and a-rollin'!"

Bren raised his gun. "These two will be in the joint being rocked and rolled."

Derek popped the trunk. "We'll mount these love-birds in here."

"No, no! Don't put me in there," Arvin cried. "I'm clau—claustro—I'm scared of small, tight spots." He sniveled while putting his hands together in a prayer gesture. "Please, sir, I'm begging you...don't put me in there, please—"

"What a blockhead!" Buford shook his noggin.

"You're lucky I'm in a good mood," Bren remarked. "Calling me sir certainly helped in my decision." He handcuffed them to a sturdy railing. "Now if you give us any trouble, even the slightest, you'll both be in the trunk."

"These handcuffs are too tight," Arvin squealed.

"Yeah, loosen them up," Buford squawked.

Russ pointed his finger. "You're bitching is totally considered the slightest trouble!"

"In other words, shut the hell up!" Derek raised his open hand.

Russ hit it with a high-five. "Like, you've so got that right!"

Derek grinned at Lydia. She smiled back.

"Well, this part of our job is done," Bren stated. "It's time to help Jack and Simone."

Derek leaned into the car. "The keys are in the ignition. If those two goons don't behave, just start it and run them over."

"Are you ready, Casanova?" Bren slammed the trunk shut. "I swear Russ is rubbing off on you."

"I totally don't rub anything on him!"

198

"Ah, once in a while you do." Derek winked.

Russ grinned. "Like, sometimes twice."

Bren's face rumpled. "Yuck!"

"Yeah, man!" Derek hurled up his open hand again.

Russ whacked it with another high-five. "Like, totally!"

"I'm the one who works with a blockhead." Bren pushed by them. "No, make that two!"

Chapter 13

Henry stopped at the top of the stairs on the second floor. "Why do I have this unsettling feeling that they are in the laboratory?"

"Wherever they are, we need to find them, and quickly," Logan replied.

"Well, if you weren't slower than one of our mangled victims we put in the morgue, we'd have caught them by now."

"You can stop harping on me now. I get it. I'm slower than death." Logan reached the top step. "You've obviously forgotten that I still have some shrapnel lodged deep in my—"

"Ask me if I care," Henry remarked.

"You better watch who you're being rude to before I kick you right in your—"

"As if you could lift your leg that high."

"If I am mad enough I can."

"Can you just follow me?"

"Yes, I'll be right behind you."

Henry halted in front of two large doors. One, which was ajar, had a sign that read: NO UNAUTHORIZED PERSONNEL. "They're in here." He pushed it open.

The lights were on as both men walked around.

"It doesn't seem they're here," Logan spoke.

Henry put his finger to his pursed lips. "Shhh..." He pointed to an oblong counter and whispered, "Behind there."

Logan nodded.

As Henry crept along one side, Jack and Simone darted out from behind a cart and ran into a nearby room. They slammed the door shut, secured it and hid behind a small counter.

"There's no way out." Henry sniggered. "I think they just signed their death warrants."

"With their own blood."

Henry lifted his pistol, aimed and blew off several rounds until the door lurched open. "Look Logan," he warbled. "We've been invited inside."

"Remind me to tip the doorman."

"I shall," Henry said. "Let's tend to the guests."

They both scuttled in and kept low to the ground.

"I know you're in here, so show yourselves," Henry growled.

"Your issue is with me," Jack stated. "Let her go."

Henry grunted. "Are you referring to media darling, Simone Wellington?"

"Prescott, she has nothing to do with this," Jack retorted. "If you've got any hope of this ending well then just let her go."

"Mr. Stanwick, are you suggesting I give up one of my bargaining chips?"

"All I'm saying is somebody in this room wants to be the next President," Jack replied. "Maybe the Secretary of State can reason with you. After all, Mr. Price has so much more to lose than you do."

Logan sighed. "Maybe we should weigh our options."

"Here are your options..." Henry barked, grabbing him by his lapel. "One will be your death! The other is you will never be the President of the United States—not now—not ever! The only place you will be presiding over is the Big House with an eight-by-twelve cell as the Lincoln bedroom and a guy named Bubba as your First Lady. What's your choice?"

Logan scowled. "I'd rather not choose."

"Wrong choice!" Henry squawked. "I'm trying to get us out of this alive." The spit flew from his mouth. "I'll never survive in prison, so we either choose this, or we die."

Jack came out from behind the counter. "Prescott, drop your weapon! I said drop your weapon!"

Henry bent down and placed his gun on the floor.

"Now drop to your knees and clasp your hands behind your head," Jack commanded. "Mr. Price, do the same."

Logan assumed the position. "Mr. Stanwick, just name your price."

Jack kicked the gun aside. "I want a hundred for each of you."

"A hundred thousand dollars?" Henry reacted.

Jack chuckled. "A hundred years for each at a federal penitentiary!"

Without warning, a shot rang out, propelling him against the counter. The gun soared from his hand and landed under a chair next to the wall. "Damn it," he yelled out, bringing the bleeding hand to his lips.

Logan laughed and stood to his feet. "Didn't know I had one of these babies, huh, Mr. FBI agent?" He held the gun steady. "Probably also didn't know that I'm a card-carrying member of the NRA and have a High Masters, or that I received the Bright Wreath Medal in sharpshooting in 2000 then the Beacon-Booker trophy in pistol shooting in 2003? Not to mention my many medals in archery, but why show-off? You've gotten the point!"

Jack kept the wounded hand in his mouth and said nothing.

Henry went over, picked up the gun and turned to Logan. "Go get the girl while I keep an eye on this fool."

He hurried away.

"Well, Mr. Stanwick..." Henry grinned. "You don't mind if I call you Jack?" He waved the gun. "Ah, even if you do, who gives a crap? I'm the one calling the shots."

"Stop pulling away," Logan shouted.

"Let go of me!" Simone screamed.

"Who are you to make demands?" Logan hollered. "I'm the one with the gun."

"Jack, I'm so sorry..." Simone's eyes swelled with tears. "It's all my fault!"

"Settle down," Henry bellowed. "After all, this is a place of business."

"Simone, please..." Jack pleaded. "Do as they say."

"Smart boy," Henry remarked. "The FBI has taught you well." He glared at her. "Your boyfriend makes a valid point."

She shrank back.

"That's much better." Logan stroked the pistol against the side of her face.

Simone pulled away.

"What're we going to do with them?" Logan inquired. "Not that I can't think of something to do with this lovely creature."

"Enough!" Henry growled. "C'mon, follow me." He grabbed Jack and held the gun to his head. "We're going to have us a little party."

"Let's go, sweetheart," Logan snarled.

After dragging their hostages to the far end of the laboratory, Henry stopped.

"Here, take my gun," he said through gritted teeth.

Logan grasped it by the handle.

"I need to get the party favors." Henry walked up to a large counter and reached up to a cupboard door. After opening it, he collected several items, brought them back to the group and dropped them on a table.

"What're you up to?" Logan questioned.

"Give me both the guns!" Henry insisted.

"Sure." Logan passed them off.

"I want you to take that bundle of twine off the table and tie their hands together behind their backs," Henry ordered. "Then take a couple of rags and shove them into their mouths. Up to this point, they've had nothing of importance to offer me, and the last thing I want to hear now is needless drivel."

Logan completed the task.

"Now position Mr. Stanwick and Ms. Wellington so they're facing each other, and then wrap the rest of the twine securely around them." Henry directed. "When you're done, tie the ends into several taut knots."

Once Logan finished the job, he stated, "It would take a pair of hedge trimmers to cut this off."

"Good, now hold these..." Henry handed off the guns. "And don't take your eyes off them, especially him."

"Why?" Logan asked. "They're bound and gagged. He's going nowhere."

"Never turn your back on your enemy," Henry retorted. "And certainly not on one who works for the government. Being the Secretary of State, you of all people should know that."

"True." Logan looked toward Jack.

Henry took a set of keys out of his front pocket.

"What are those for?"

"What's a party without some drinks?" Henry sneered. "It's time to break out the Prescott family brew."

Logan grinned. "Where are you storing it these days?"

"The same place I keep all of my valuables," came the snooty reply. "Inside my father's customized safe."

Logan nodded.

Henry left the room and entered his private workspace. Hanging on the far wall was a vast painting of his wife. He grabbed hold of the right side, opened it then turned a dial on the robust door. Once cracked, he retrieved several items, placed them on a tray and went back into the laboratory.

"I wasn't gone too long, or was I?" He clutched a labeled bottle of TB4711 and shook it. "I wouldn't want my guests to become bored."

Logan snickered. "No, as a matter of fact, Simone will mention our soiree on the front page of her rag."

"How wonderful, and in the society section no less." Henry unscrewed the cap and poured the formula into two beakers with a steady hand. Amid a one-footed turn, he walked over to his accomplice. "Remove the rags." The command was given.

"Yes, sir!" Logan thrust a salute to his forehead. He marched toward the joined captives and took the gags out of their mouths.

"Jack, I'm so sorry," Simone cried, her eyes brimming over with fresh tears. "I'm so sorry!"

"It's my fault." He welled up. "I involved you." A stray drop trickled alongside his nose. "I had such a hard time saying no to you."

She sobbed as black streams gushed from her mascara-laden lashes. "I just wanted to be near you."

Jack nuzzled his cheek against her head. "Me too."

"Can we stop with the dramatics?" Henry huffed. "Damn! You'd think you were after an Academy Award."

Logan laughed. "They won't need one where they're going."

"You're both going to hell!" Simone screeched.

"Calm down, dear," Henry uttered. "I want you to be of sound mind when you see your boyfriend's transformation."

"Leave her alone!" Jack roared, thrashing against the twine. "I'll kill you, Prescott, if you harm her."

Henry stepped back. "Why Mr. Stanwick, it seems you've gotten your panties in a wad."

"I mean it!" Jack snapped with spit spurting out of his mouth.

"Watch who you're threatening, Mr. Stanwick," Henry croaked, grabbing a fistful of hair. "Let's see if this will take the piss and vinegar out of you!" He lifted the beaker. "Open your mouth now and take a swig of this."

"Finally, I can see the formula at work," Logan stated.

Jack jerked his head back.

Henry shoved the bottle into the FBI agent's lips. "Drink it!"

Simone lunged forward and sunk her teeth into her captor's hand, causing him to drop the caustic solution.

205

"You bitch!" Henry let go of Jack's hair. "Grab me another beaker of formula," he growled, glaring at her. "You'll now drink it first. I've always wanted to see what it would do to a woman."

Logan poured another and brought it over.

"Any last words?" Henry sneered.

Simone's tear-stained face edged toward Jack. With her lips trembling, she said, "I love you."

His head drooped. "I love you too."

Simultaneously, as if of one mind, their lips locked in a formidable kiss.

Henry grabbed her hair and yanked, but she wouldn't let go. He latched onto their foreheads and pushed with all of his might. When that didn't work, he turned to his accomplice. "Slug him in the face as hard as you can."

Logan secured his footing on a step ladder, balled up his hand then pulled back his arm. With a powerful thud, he himself hit the floor.

Russ stood over him and grinned. He threw another punch that knocked the Secretary of State unconscious.

Henry was startled by the ambush and spun around, only to feel Derek's sturdy fist hit him square in the jaw.

Bren whipped out his Swiss Army knife and ran over to the hostages. "I was a Boy Scout," he clamored while severing the twine. Within seconds, they were freed.

Jack and Simone wrapped their arms around each other and hugged tight.

Bren closed the blade of his knife. "Well, my work here is done."

"Like, so is mine." Russ slapped Logan in the face to wake him up.

"I can't believe we're still alive!" Simone declared.

Jack chuckled. "I'm just glad I'm still a guy!"

"Hey, can you not rub it in?" Derek quipped as he hoisted a handcuffed Henry to his feet.

206

"Sorry, guys!" Jack kicked the tattered twine aside. "I should be thanking you for saving our lives."

"Yes, we both should," Simone added. "I'll make sure to give our heroes a grateful, thank you, on the front page of my newspaper."

"In capital letters?" Bren asked.

Simone picked up her purse and smiled. "In bold capital letters!"

"Dudes, really?" Russ blurted out. "Like, aren't we undercover detectives?" he uttered, emphasizing the word undercover.

At that moment, sirens could be heard in the distance.

"Oh, yeah..." Derek smirked. "I forgot we started a little fire." He chirped. "That's why we're sort of wet."

"A fire!" Jack croaked. "Will somebody grab that dark bottle on the tray?" He pointed to the counter. "The formula you guys were exposed to is in it."

"I'll get that," Bren reacted.

Jack and Simone ran out of the laboratory as the detectives followed, dragging their handcuffed prisoners along. They rushed out the front doors to safety.

A fire truck rounded the chain-link fence with its sirens blaring as an emergency vehicle trailed behind.

"Where's our car?" Derek tried catching his breath.

"The broad drove off in it," Arvin replied. "That is, after yelling out the window that she dumped Logan."

"I said that we shouldn't have hired a woman," Buford groused.

"That bitch!" Logan snapped. "Lydia stole some of the formula and put it into a perfume bottle. She's going back to France to get revenge on some man who jilted her."

"Like, let me call her." Russ pulled out his cell phone and dialed the number. "It totally went to voicemail."

"Man, I can't believe she would leave us in this hellhole," Derek whined.

"Dudes, I've only got one blinking bar left—"

"Then shut it off," Derek countered.

207

"At least you've got a cell phone," Bren grumbled. "Ours are in the duffle bags that are burning up as we speak."

Derek sneered. "It gives a whole new meaning to burner phones."

Jack's cell phone rang. He stepped aside, reached into his jacket pocket and pulled it out. "Hello?"

"Hey, it's Blaine. I'm finally finished with all the paperwork on the Yarborough case. I can help you now."

"Ah!" Jack puffed. "I've just wrapped up the case with help from the guys at the Davenport Detective Agency."

"Great," Blaine stated. "I'm glad."

"So, you're not upset that the case was solved without you?"

"Not at all," came his reply. "As a matter of fact, I'll finally get the chance to crack a case or two on my own."

"What're you talking about?"

"Since it was solely your investigation, imagine all the paperwork you'll have to complete on your own..." He explained. "I had no involvement whatsoever, and you can't let on that the detectives were really hired by you."

"Damn it!" Jack groaned. "I forgot about that."

"I'll talk with you in a month," Blaine said. "See ya!"

"Don't wanna be ya!" Jack shook his head as he hung up the cell phone.

"Is there anything I can do to help?" Simone asked.

"Would you give the guys a ride home?" He leaned in. "I've got to wait for the transport unit to pick up these humps."

She smiled. "Sure, it would be my pleasure."

"It'd way be mine too," Russ uttered. "I so call shotgun."

"Ah, no you won't!" Jack declared. "You'll for sure be riding in the backseat."

Russ nodded. "Like, totally."

"You're such an idiot." Bren pushed him.

208

"Guys, follow me. I need to say something." Jack pulled the detectives aside. "After Raymond told me about your predicament, I called in some favors to get all your current and subsequent medical bills paid courtesy of the FBI. Our shrinks are also available to speak with at any time; twenty-four hours a day, so don't hesitate to use them for as long as you guys need them. It goes without saying that anything—and I do mean anything—that you guys need, just let me know."

The detectives nodded in silence.

"The three of you will never be fully recognized for your bravery or the great sacrifices you've made to save the President, but know this one thing..." Jack cleared his throat. "I am here, and always will be." When the emotional acknowledgement finished, he gave each man a firm handshake and a heartfelt hug.

"Like, look on the bright side..." Russ grinned. "You'll totally have twice as many detectives to help out on your next big case."

Jack chuckled. "Sounds great, but there'll be no bartering for higher pay."

Simone walked up to them.

Derek grabbed Russ by the arm. "C'mon your extreme blondness..." He pulled him away. "Let's leave them so they can talk in peace."

"Good idea," Bren reacted.

"Who wants to start my car?" Simone held up a ring of keys.

The detectives turned around and threw up their hands.

"Here they come!" She tossed them into the air.

Derek and Russ dove toward the keys as they fell to the ground and wrestled about until exhaustion set in. While huffing and puffing, they both rolled onto their backs to see Bren shaking the set of keys.

"You're both losers!" He sneered.

"Guys," Jack barked as he put his arm around Simone's waist. "Thanks for everything!"

"Like, you're so totally welcome," all three yelled back in unison. They laughed while pushing and shoving each other toward the car.

"What a great bunch of guys," Simone said.

209

"The greatest!" Jack watched them getting into the car. "Just watch out for Russ." He nuzzled up to her. "He fancies himself a Casanova."

"Not to worry, he's riding in the backseat."

"That might not deter him."

"Well, if not, he will be put out of the car and have to hitch a ride home."

"I'm just glad everything came off without a hitch." Jack stared into her eyes.

"Speaking of hitched..." Simone fussed with his jacket lapel. "Will I see you again?"

"Well, we still have a newspaper article to contend with," he responded. "I did agree to a no-holds-barred interview. I'm no journalist, but I assume something of that magnitude could last hours, or days...maybe even weeks—"

"Or several months," Simone added, reaching into her handbag. "Here, I sort of picked this up." She handed him a neatly gift-wrapped item.

"What's this for?"

"You'll see."

Jack ripped it open. "Wow, a leather wallet!" His face beamed as he pecked her on the cheek. "Thank you."

Simone touched the side of her face then lunged forward to plant a whopper of a kiss on his lips. She purred when finished. "You're welcome."

Jack exhaled. "We'll definitely be getting together tomorrow."

Arm in arm, he walked her to the car and opened the door.

"Until tomorrow..." She smooched him then sat down. "Goodbye."

"Bye." Jack closed her door.

Simone waved as she drove away.

Chapter 14

Lydia drove up to the Alabaster Hotel and slammed on the brakes. With the engine running, she jumped out of the car, ran across the lobby and pushed the elevator button several times.

Please, move faster!

Her foot tapped continuously until it arrived. Once the doors opened, she hopped on and went to the sixth floor. When it stopped, Lydia ran to her room, grabbed a few suitcases and threw them on the immaculate bed.

They covered over the dirty secret with clean sheets. I will have to leave housekeeping a tip.

Lydia grasped the wallet from her handbag, pulled out some cash and left it on the nightstand.

Now I need to call a bellboy.

She clutched the phone and pushed a button.

"Hello, would you please send somebody up to bring my luggage down to the car?"

Lydia hung up the phone and hastily jam-packed her belongings. She dragged everything into the entryway and patiently waited.

Finally, there was a knock on the door.

She peeked through the peephole then flung it open.

"Hello, I'm Jake," the young guy said. "I was sent to take your bags down."

"Yes, please!" Lydia nodded then stepped aside.

211

The bellboy hauled the baggage onto a cart. When finished, he wheeled them to her vehicle, packed it all in the trunk and closed it. "Thank you!" Lydia handed him some money then slid behind the steering wheel and peeled away.

When I get home, people will pay for humiliating me. Her face scowled as she weaved in and out of traffic.

A horn honked, and then another.

"Excuse me, but I have an appointment with revenge," Lydia yelled out. "And I cannot be late!

She sped down State Road 267, pulled alongside the curb at Washington Dulles International Airport and stopped. Lydia hopped out of the car, opened the trunk then ran up to the baggage valet. "Would you gather my suitcases and follow me, please?"

"Sure," he replied. The valet placed everything on a luggage cart and trailed behind her.

Lydia hurried through the sliding glass doors and waited in line for an AirFrance agent. When it became her turn, she headed to the counter. "When is the next flight leaving for Paris?"

A woman tapped the keys on her computer. "It's scheduled for departure in two and half hours." She looked up. "Shall I reserve a seat?"

"Yes, please!" With her face beaming, Lydia reached for her wallet.

After purchasing a ticket, she passed through security, walked to the departing gate and found a seat.

I feel bad not saying goodbye to my friend. Let me call her. Lydia grabbed the cell phone from her handbag and dialed it.

A generic voicemail was heard. "Hello, Rue," she said with a sad tone. "I am so sorry for dashing away without a word. I have a family emergency and need to leave for France. I will talk with you soon."

As her call ended, it was time to board. Lydia got onto the plane and sat down in her assigned seat next to a little old lady.

"Hello, dear!"

Lydia smiled.

212

"My name is Mae Belle Grafton," the woman said in a frail and shaking voice. "What is yours?"

"I am Lydia Reome."

"You have such a lovely French accent."

"Why, thank you."

"Was your stay in Washington, DC for business or pleasure?"

Lydia smirked. "It was a little of both." Her head tilted. "Are you vacationing in Paris?"

"I'm visiting my granddaughter in Mourmont," Mae Belle answered as a glint came to her eyes. "I haven't seen her in quite some time."

"You will love the countryside, especially this time of the year." Lydia gleamed. "The colors are so beautiful and vibrant. I think this week the leaves are at peak—"

"Hello and welcome!" A booming voice sounded over the loudspeaker. "My name is Captain Jenkins and our copilot is Captain Reynolds. Your flight attendants today are Dena and Marie, and they'll take very good care of you. We're currently third in line for takeoff, so please, remain seated with your seatbelts fastened.

Our flight time should be about eight hours and sixteen minutes. The cruising speed, depending on where you live, will be 804 kilometers or 500 miles per hour, at an altitude of 35,000 feet, so sit back, relax and have a pleasant flight."

After the flight attendants gave the regulatory safety spiel, the airplane began to taxi down the runway and moved faster with every bounce. Before they knew it, the passengers were air-bound, soaring over a beautifully lit Washington, DC. Refreshments were served when the desired elevation was achieved.

"Although it has been some time, I quite enjoy flying," the little old lady shared. "The feeling of being suspended in air is absolutely wonderful."

Lydia shuddered. "I have not been able to enjoy it since the time my father's friend took me up on a small two-seater plane, the type that looks like a crop duster."

"What happened?"

213

"As soon as we took flight, the thing was spattering and sputtering all over the place with puffs of smoke shooting out the backend. It was only when it began rolling from side to side that I became quite ill." Lydia held her stomach. "Then out of nowhere, it dropped elevation and shook so violently that we had to make an emergency landing. I was frightened to death—"

"Oh, my!" Mae Belle expressed.

"Oh, my, is right," Lydia quipped. "I grabbed the door handle and asked if we were going to crash and die. The pilot snickered and stated, 'Nonsense, I could land this baby with one arm tied behind my back.' Well, after what seemed like an eternity, he finally landed it, but broke his arm in the process. I myself had several lacerations on my arms and legs that required stitches. At the hospital, he came into the room where I was being treated with a cast on. I stared him in the eyes and said, 'I guess now you can properly test your one arm theory, but this time, without me.'" She leaned back and exhaled. "This is the second time I have been on a plane since the crash."

"How are you feeling?"

"I think the anxiety is affecting my stomach." Lydia rummaged around in her handbag. "Maybe a piece of gum will help."

"I have some chewable tablets for motion sickness," the little old lady offered. "I bought them for just this occasion." She pulled out a small square pill box, opened it and handed one to her.

"Thank you!" Lydia took the orange pill and tossed it into her mouth.

"I noticed you had a perfume bottle in your purse," Mae Belle remarked. "What kind do you wear?"

Lydia flinched as she looked down. *Quickly, think of something.* "What you had seen was a prototype of a new fragrance my company is working on." She shoved it deeper into her handbag. "I am a researcher for a cosmetics company."

"May I try it on?"

"We have not finalized the formula," Lydia responded. "It still causes a burning sensation followed by a rash."

The little old lady put a hand to her cheek. "Oh, my heavens!"

With a quick jolt, the airplane rattled and caused Lydia to scream out. She clutch her seat, gasping for air as the vessel quavered.

"Ladies and gentlemen," the PA system clattered. "This is Captain Jenkins. We are experiencing some turbulence. Please, remain seated with your seatbelts fastened."

"There, there, my dear." Mae Belle tapped Lydia's hand. "See, you have nothing to worry about."

"I guess not." She eased her grip on the armrest. "My nerves are a little on edge."

"No apology needed, dear."

Lydia rubbed her stomach. "I am still feeling somewhat nauseous."

"Maybe it's not motion sickness."

"Then what else could it be?"

"Could you be pregnant?"

"That is impossible!" Lydia shooed the idea away with a swish of her hand.

"Oh, my, did I offend you?" Mae Belle placed a hand against her chest.

"No, of course not," Lydia reacted. "I just need to relax a bit." She stretched out. "I am sure it will go away soon."

"You're probably right," the little old lady said as she turned toward the window.

Lydia rested her head against the seat and closed her eyes. *Pregnant!* She laughed to herself. *Wait a minute...* The eyes opened. *What if I am? And if so, by which man?*